NIGHT
ROAD

Also by A. M. Jenkins

Breaking Boxes

Damage

Out of Order

Beating Heart: A Ghost Story

Repossessed

NIGHT ROAD

A. M. Jenkins

HARPER TEEN
An Imprint of HarperCollinsPublishers

To Phyllis Reynolds Naylor, for her immense
kindness and generosity

HarperTeen is an imprint of HarperCollins Publishers.

Night Road

Copyright © 2008 by A. M. Jenkins

www.harperteen.com

Library of Congress Cataloging-in-Publication Data is available.
ISBN 978-0-06-054604-5 (trade bdg.)—ISBN 978-0-06-054605-2 (lib. bdg.)

Typography by Joel Tippie
2 3 4 5 6 7 8 9 10
❖
First Edition

ACKNOWLEDGMENTS

I am humbly grateful to Marthe Jocelyn, Robert Lipsyte, and Norma Fox Mazer for their ability to look at a working draft of eighty pages and see past its flaws to its possibilities.

I would also like to clone Rex Naylor and distribute him to all writers in need of a supportive spouse.

PART ONE

The Building

CHAPTER ONE

COLE *did* have a map in his backpack. He'd studied it in the parking garage. Only now that he was already on the subway did it occur to him that it might be outdated.

What a foolish mistake on his part, to assume that he could rely on a thirty-year-old map.

Cole loathed mistakes.

Next stop—*Fifth Avenue*? That couldn't be right. Fifth was on the wrong side of the park, wasn't it?

He'd decided to take the train into Manhattan because he'd had difficulty once when he'd taken a cab. The stop-and-start traffic had made him carsick, which had been very unpleasant for both him and the cab-driver, who had neither seen nor smelled regurgitated blood before. And of course, as soon as his stomach was emptied, he had to prevent the Thirst that would inevitably follow. He'd quickly fed on the cabdriver, a hairy man who apparently was not fond of bathing. He'd had to take more than usual; then he'd felt bad about leaving the man unconscious and tucked a large tip into the guy's shirt pocket.

Now Cole sat, feeling the muted throb of the tracks under the car, and he had an uncomfortable suspicion he was moving farther and farther away from where he needed to be.

He did not want to pull out his own map. To pull out a map and pore over it in New York City screamed "TOURIST! COME ROB ME!" But there was no help for it. He was an idiot. He should have gotten a new map and studied it before he even got out of his car.

He got off at the next stop—Lexington Avenue—backpack slung over his shoulders. He did not like using the backpack, which crushed and wrinkled the clothes inside. Of course, he had not wanted to come into the city at all—but his wants had nothing to do with it, and the backpack was less obtrusive than his suitcase, which had wheels and a handle that popped up.

Real eighteen-year-old guys, Cole felt, did not walk

alone at night wheeling luggage on the subways and streets of Manhattan.

He walked across the platform as quickly as possible and leaned with his back against the concrete wall, under the faint sterile buzz of a fluorescent light. There he pulled out the map and discreetly unfolded one corner, hoping that would be enough to give him a clue where Lexington Avenue was in the scheme of things.

It wasn't. He unfurled the whole damn thing. Fine, he was a teenage tourist.

But the map didn't make any sense. Cole didn't even know where he was. And all those colored lines branching off. Now, here he was who knew where, holding a tangled mess of lines on a paper that was worse than useless because the stupid trains didn't always stop at each station that was marked. No, they sometimes *skipped* stations, which, now that he thought about it, was likely what had happened to him. Or perhaps he'd gotten on the wrong train in the first place, back when he'd switched from the PATH train.

God. He'd have to go up, get his bearings, and walk to his destination.

Unless he was in Queens. Or any place that didn't

have streets numbered in a grid.

The problem was that he'd been too complacent. Cole had thought he already had the answers when he *knew* that the moment you let down your guard is the moment you start making mistakes. He'd just thought he could remember from the last time he'd been here. He couldn't recall the year exactly, but it was the summer Lady Di married Prince Charles. He remembered because Mina and Alice had kept Johnny's TV tuned in to the wedding.

Now, map still in hand, he headed up the concrete stairs to the sidewalk to look at street signs and figure out where he was.

He'd only stayed a few weeks during the Charles-and-Di summer. The longest Cole had ever stayed in Manhattan was for three or four years, back when Johnny had first bought the Building; but that was before the subways had been extended this far.

At the top of the steps Cole paused, map in his hand. It had rained recently, but not much. The air was damp and heavy and smelled of wet streets and steamy concrete, but the only water was a trickle in the gutters, a darker patch here and there on the sidewalk.

Not far away, under the corner street sign, some guy in a greasy overcoat was dancing in the middle of the sidewalk, flapping his arms slowly, his eyes on an invisible somebody right in front of him.

"Code red, Code red," Cole heard him announce to the somebody. "Frequency forty-nine has been alerted. Clearance requested from the emperor."

All right. There was no hurry; it was several hours till dawn. And Cole did not know why Johnny had called him in, but if it had been urgent, there was no question that Johnny would have told him so.

Of course, he had not tried to find out what it was all about. He'd felt a vague discomfort licking at him, but rather than ask Johnny why he wanted him to come in, Cole had asked instead: *Is everything all right?* And Johnny had said yes.

Anything beyond that, he knew, could wait.

He peered at the strange man again—he could almost smell the stale odor of unwashed clothes from here. He wasn't afraid of the guy, just reluctant to get involved in a hassle out on a public street.

"Need help?"

Cole turned. It was a woman. Not hemovore. An

omnivore. You could always tell even if no bodily movements gave it away. An omni's eyes had a stunted, undeveloped look, while a heme's gaze was ripe to the core. This omni woman had short gray hair, wore jeans, and carried a canvas bag looped over one shoulder.

"I'm lost," Cole admitted. He hoped she was not a mugger. He hated the way muggers reacted when they shot him badly and he didn't fall down. He hated it even more when they shot him well and he did.

"Where are you trying to go?" She sounded matter-of-fact, but she stayed just out of reach; she wasn't completely stupid. Only partially so, helping a stranger at night.

He took one more look at the useless map, then crumpled it up into a ball and dropped it into a trash can next to the railing. "I'm trying to get to West One Hundred and Second." He put his hands in his pockets so it wouldn't look as if he were about to grab her. Then it occurred to him that she might think he was digging for a weapon, so he took his hands out. Then he wasn't sure what to do with them.

He ended up clasping them in front of him like a fig leaf. He hated New York.

"You need to take the V train back to Rockefeller Center, then catch the B. I'm pretty sure it stops at One Hundred and Third. You can get off and walk from there."

"Okay." Cole had no idea what she'd just said. "Thank you." He decided he'd find a cab and just hope it was a short ride.

"No problem." She tugged the bag up over her shoulder and had started to turn away when Cole spoke.

"Listen," he said. "You shouldn't approach strangers at night. It's not wise."

She paused but didn't stop. "I knew it was okay," she called over her shoulder. "You have kind eyes. And you're wearing a cross."

He looked down. He always wore the necklace under his shirt, but sometimes it worked its way out to dangle in full view. It *was* a cross, made of two nails bound together with wire.

He dropped it back inside his collar so that it hung against his skin. By the time he looked up, the woman was gone, disappeared down the stairs as if swept away by a current. He stood looking after her for a second, knowing he'd never see her again. That's the way it always was; he stood still while everyone else got swallowed up and lost.

Luckily, he saw a taxi down the street dropping off two people; and as he raised his hand and started toward it, he wondered again just why Johnny had asked him to come back.

CHAPTER TWO

IT was past four in the morning by the time Cole was buzzed into a hallway that smelled faintly of wax and polish. His sneakers made no noise on the tiled floor.

Cole ignored the first door—it was no longer used—and went directly to the one at the back. Johnny's apartment took up the two bottom floors.

A lanky guy with a flop of red hair let him in. It was Mitch—laid-back, easygoing Mitch. "Hey, Cole," he said, unsurprised. His face was friendly. "Long time no see."

"Mitchell."

"Come on in, man. How're the boondocks?"

"Amazing," Cole answered, stepping into the apartment. "The people actually wait for the lights to change before trying to cross the street."

"Uh-huh," said Mitch, undisturbed. "Well, Johnny's out back."

Of course Johnny would be out there. He spent most evenings on the patio, until it got cold. And most of the other hemes would be with him. What they did, mostly, was sit around talking, exactly like some of the suburban omnis Cole had seen hanging out in their yards in the summer, chatting while their kids played hide-and-seek or football.

Cole considered. He was thoroughly out of sorts after the stupid subway—out of patience, out of energy.

But he ought to check in, see what was going on.

"I'll just go put my things up," he told Mitch, not moving from the door. "Then I'll come on out."

"Whatever floats your boat," Mitch said cheerfully. "Johnny said you could have four-and-a-half. Do you want a feed?"

Cole did not like open feeding; he was out of the habit, and it made him uncomfortable. But he always took a feed when it was available—that was only wise, to keep desire from taking recognizable form so that it would never, ever turn into need. "Just a small bit," he told Mitch reluctantly.

"Sure. Gotcha. Just give me a sec." And Mitch disappeared through the swinging door that led into the kitchen.

Cole looked around the apartment. Most of the furniture had changed since the last time he was here. The white rugs were new. And those overstuffed chairs—they were new too. The couch was leather now. A flat-screen TV hung on the wall, tuned to ESPN.

The place was large, for Manhattan. The door next to the television led to the kitchen—a real kitchen, Cole knew, that you could walk around in. In the corner a spiral staircase led to the second-floor bedrooms. Next to that, a small hallway. And across the living room, a sliding glass door led to the patio. Cole could see movement outside.

He couldn't put his finger on any one thing about Johnny's apartment that made him uncomfortable. It was welcoming and clean. You could discuss an art exhibit or watch a football game and not feel out of place. You could feed anytime you wanted, take naps on the couch, never worry about sun. Everyone was safe here; everyone who entered was insulated from risk, from extremes.

And, after all, was that such a bad thing?

Mitch came back, pulling an omni by the hand. It was a girl with her eyes heavily outlined in black, her dyed-black hair framed on one side in red, the other in purple. Of course she wore black. The Building omnis almost always did.

Cole smiled automatically—his smile was one of his weapons—but it wasn't necessary, because she held out her hand with a flourish. Her eyes stayed on him as he slowly took her hand in his. Mitch didn't leave, or turn away—he just stood there watching the basketball game, apparently waiting for Cole to finish.

This was, after all, the Building. Open feeding was an everyday occurrence.

Cole turned the omni's hand over and lifted her wrist. There were scars on it, small circles healed and half healed. This, too, was something he was unused to. He pulled out the necklace hidden under his shirt and gently punctured her skin with one of the nails.

He watched her face as he fed. There they went— the eyes, growing dazed, unfocused. Most of the time, on the road, you didn't get to see their faces. He hadn't forgotten what it was like, the slow tease of open feeding—but he'd put it out of his mind.

Now her eyelids grew heavy, half shut. Her lips relaxed

and parted. Her breath seemed to unwind from some-where beneath her breasts, escaping in a heavy sigh.

That's what happened to them; they got lost in a haze of pleasure and well-being, like flies doped into paralysis by a spider. Watching them certainly added another dimension to the whole experience. It became about more than just sustenance when you could see their faces.

The danger was in getting caught up in it. When she swayed on her feet, Cole realized that he had fed longer than usual, enjoying the moment.

The Building could do that to you in just a few seconds.

He lifted his head, the small cut in her skin ceasing to bleed in the same instant. He watched as the girl's eyes began to focus. He did not release her hand, wait-ing to make sure she was steady on her feet. "Do you need to sit down?" he asked.

She shook her head.

"Well," Cole said. "Thank you."

"Thank *you*." She looked speculatively up at him. "I'm Mary Kate. And *you're* cute. Going to be around for a while?"

"I'm not sure." Cole turned to Mitch. "Can I have that key now?"

"Um?" Mitch tore his gaze away from the television.

"Sure. Right." He reached to a rack by the door and pulled off a key. "Here. Four-and-a-half. Give a shout if you need anything."

"Thanks, I will. See you in a few."

"Good deal."

"Want any company?" Mary Kate asked.

"Thank you," said Cole, "but no."

"Later?"

"I—I don't know." The omnis here were almost like groupies. "I have some things to do. And I'm a little tired; I've been on the road all night."

"Okay," she said reluctantly. "But I got to you first, so you have to pick me if you want anything. Promise?"

"Yes. I promise."

Out in the hall he boarded the elevator. It was oddly shaped, small and elongated so that two passengers had to stand shoulder to shoulder facing the door.

Cole, of course, was alone. He pressed the button for the fourth floor and waited.

And waited.

And waited.

Finally, with a painful lurch, the elevator rose and began to thrum slowly upward. It would have been quicker to take the stairs.

He had always felt an odd affection for this awful piece of machinery, lumbering on like a faithful ox pulling its plow decade after decade. For the first time, he felt pleased to be in New York.

As the elevator door opened on the fourth floor, he heard piano music.

Cole got out. The music came from one of the fourth-floor apartments. Probably Elise. She lived elsewhere in the city, but came here to practice every night.

The elevator only went to the fourth floor. Apartment four-and-a-half was on a landing carved into the middle of the long staircase between four and five—a mere blip in the stairs. The apartments farther up were not often used, he knew, except for one at the back of the building.

He trudged up the stairs with his backpack, then hesitated on the landing. He turned his head and looked up toward the fifth floor.

A light shone at the top of the stairs. For a brief moment he considered walking up and knocking on the door of that one apartment.

He only held on to the thought for a second or two

before putting it aside. There was no point in going up there. It wouldn't do any good. It wouldn't even be noticed.

He knew Johnny's request had nothing to do with the fifth floor. Everything would always be the same up there.

So he unlocked the door to four-and-a-half and walked in. Four-and-a-half had two bedrooms and no living room. The shower trickled mostly cold water, and the kitchen was the size of a bathtub. He was quite familiar with four-and-a-half. He usually ended up staying in it when he was here.

He unpacked, then sorted his laundry; tomorrow night he would take advantage of the washer and dryer in the basement.

Finally, he was ready. He locked the door carefully behind him and rode the ancient elevator down.

This time he did not knock at the door of Johnny's apartment but walked right in.

CHAPTER THREE

MITCH was still there, stretched out in a plush armchair that just about enveloped him. All that could be seen were his long legs extending over the carpet and a shock of red hair. He poked his head up to see who had come in, then waved at Cole and informed him, "Lakers, 52–45, halftime," before pushing the shock of hair back and fastening his gaze on the TV again.

Three omnis now sat in the overstuffed chairs, shoes kicked off onto the carpet. They were talking quietly and did not see Cole come in. The sliding glass door to the patio was open just a crack. It had been—what, twenty-five, thirty years since he'd seen any of the New York hemes?

Cole walked alone to the door. He did not touch the glass, but paused, looking through at the patio outside.

It was the closest thing to a yard most of Manhattan had to offer: a brick patio edged with flower beds, a strip of grass along the back fence. A dozen or so people sat around, some on cushioned iron furniture, some on wooden dining chairs that had been brought outside. White lanterns hung in a line over the bricks, and low, dim lights lit the edges of the patio.

It looked much as it always had. These people had always been here, every night, making the petty decisions that enabled the Colony to exist, taking care of mundane chores and daily responsibilities.

For all those years Cole had been taking care of only himself.

". . . the intricate details." A languid voice floated in through the open door. "The innuendoes that underlie mezzo-forte—"

That was Frederick, holding forth on the exact same subject he'd been holding forth on a quarter of a century ago. And there was Johnny, thin and small, pale hair buzzed short. And Cole saw the other NYC hemes, the ones who came to the Building almost nightly.

There was Nell, still peering at people through her glasses. Alice, with a stack of papers in her lap—Alice was Johnny's go-to girl; she kept track of all the IDs and credit cards, and knew more about Colony business than anyone, perhaps even Johnny himself. Mina, with blonde hair now—hadn't it been auburn last time?—nodding eagerly, waiting for a chance to add her opinions.

For a moment Cole felt as though he were seeing them as a stranger would, all of them with unlined faces and youthful bodies. If you didn't look into their eyes, if you didn't notice the way they moved, not one of them appeared to be more than twenty-one or two.

Of course, some of the omnis really *were* young. There were several of them on the patio. Generally the omnis in the Building were young people who read too much Anne Rice, and once they were here, they usually stayed.

The ones on the patio wouldn't be out there for long, Cole knew, not after he stepped outside and the discussion got started. Johnny did not allow the omnis to participate in Colony business. All in all, Cole thought they had it pretty good. They weren't allowed the freedom they'd have had on their own, perhaps—Johnny allowed no alcohol or drugs in the Building, no friends dropping by—but on the other hand they had everything they needed and most things they wanted, with almost no responsibilities.

And they got the glorious dreams they craved. That was why most of them never wanted to leave.

"Cole?" said a voice behind him.

Cole turned. "Seth!" Seth had finally cut off his ponytail. He'd been loath to part with it since he'd been able to regrow it in the sixties.

They shook hands. "It's been a while," Seth said. "When did you get in?"

"Just a bit ago."

"You been outside yet?"

"Not yet."

Seth glanced out through the glass. Frederick's voice came wafting into the apartment. ". . . the power behind the pianissimo . . ."

"I don't blame you," Seth said.

". . . also, I thought the breathing and the phrasing lacked unity . . ."

"I was wanting to talk to you when you got in anyway," Seth told Cole. "I wish you'd start carrying a phone."

"No, thanks."

"Then at least get a laptop. That way you can keep in touch better."

"Just one more thing to lug around."

"No, I'm serious. It's perfect—I know you like your privacy, but with email you don't have to talk to anybody, and you can answer in your own sweet time. We never know where you are. If you want, I could look into it and find one—"

Whump! The swinging door to the kitchen flew open.

Cole and Seth turned to see a boy come in. There was a girl plastered to his side; one of his arms was slung carelessly around her shoulders as he paused awkwardly to still the noisy flap of the door.

The girl was obviously omni. But the boy?

He had the intense gaze of a heme—but his eyes wouldn't settle on anything long enough to really observe it. He didn't seem to notice Cole and Seth. And he moved with too much energy.

"Who is that?" Cole asked Seth.

"Gordon."

"Guerdon?" Cole echoed, confused. He'd had a brother named Guerdon.

"Gordon," Seth told Cole. "Our most recent accident."

23

"Oh." An accident. Someone had lost control and killed without meaning to. It didn't happen often. "It's been a while."

"Yes. I think Mitch was the last. Fifty-six or fifty-seven, I believe."

"Who, um . . . ?" Cole asked, curious.

"Sandor."

"Sandor?" It was impossible that anyone as experienced as Sandor could make a mistake like killing in the feed. Something out of the ordinary had to have caused it—but what? "Is he here now?"

"He stepped out for a feed," Seth said. "He should be back anytime."

Cole nodded. Honest, good-hearted Sandor. It would be worth this trip to see his old friend.

Gordon the Accident stood looking around the living room. Cole hadn't even thought about his brother, Guerdon, in many years, but now as he stared at the boy, a sudden stab of faceless memory came to him: a quick flash of a grin; long, dark hair with one rebel lock that refused to stay tied back.

He had no idea why, at this moment, his brain would choose to spit up such an archaic memory. The names

24

were similar, but Cole had met plenty of people named Gordon before. And this kid looked nothing like Guerdon. He wasn't smiling, and his hair was the color of ripe wheat, and it was short.

Gordon was merely glancing at faces, omni and heme alike, without taking the time to read them. Everything about him added up to proclaim that he was overly eager, clumsy, thoughtless. That wouldn't be his fault, though—he wouldn't have had much opportunity to develop a knack for observation and deduction, and no reason to, here in the Building.

"Sandor was on the road when this happened?" Cole asked.

"Yes. Terrible things can happen on the road," Seth said. "But we all should try to stay sharp, I suppose. Bertha just went out to travel a bit, did you know that?"

"No," Cole said. But he kept his eyes on Gordon; it was weird that his mind had flashed on that one bit of hair that always slipped loose and fell over Guerdon's forehead, getting in his eyes. "Where is she?"

"She's in Florence right now. I just had an email from her a few days ago. . . ."

Seth began to tell about the contents of Bertha's

email. Cole watched Gordon flop down onto the couch. The girl stood in front of him, hands on hips. She had waist-length hair, black leather pants, and a black bustier. As Gordon spoke to her earnestly—looking like a very large puppy, Cole thought—she sat *on* him, straddling his lap, taking his face in both hands and kissing him.

The omnis of the Colony were obedient, but they certainly weren't reserved.

Gordon wasn't exactly fighting her off, though. Their bodies were pressed full against each other.

"Does he do this often?" Cole interrupted Seth with a nod at the couple. It was not usual for someone—especially anyone so new—to behave in such an overtly sexual manner with an omni.

Seth turned to look. "Not that I've noticed," he said, casually enough, but he did not turn back to Cole, and he did not say anything else about email or Bertha. Instead, they both watched as the girl slid her hands to the back of Gordon's head and pulled his face to her neck. It disappeared under the curtain of her hair.

"How long has he been heme?" Cole asked.

"Two weeks." Seth sounded a little worried.

They both waited for Gordon to let go. After all, he had used his teeth, not a tool, and the flow of blood would be both heavy and swift.

But the girl remained absolutely still, and Gordon's face remained unseen under her long hair.

"Maybe he's just playing with her," Seth said, uneasy.

"I'm not so sure," Cole said.

And sure enough, the next moment, the girl slowly crumpled and fell to the side, unconscious.

"Shit," said Seth, stunned.

Cole was already halfway around the couch. "Get Johnny," he called to Seth.

Seth pulled the door open and stuck his head outside. Cole heard him calling to Johnny as Cole bent over the girl and gently rolled her onto her back. He pressed his fingers to her neck, feeling for a pulse. There was no blood anywhere, just a redness deep in the twin marks, like parentheses, that Gordon's teeth had made. Her pulse was faint but steady, and not too fast. He brushed her hair out of her face. She was quite pale.

Then Seth was back, and Johnny was with him.

"Hello, lad." That was all, just two words and a nod from Johnny—but it was more than enough. When

Johnny looked at you, it was a welcome as well as an appraisal. It didn't really need words.

Cole stood and moved aside to let him kneel next to the girl.

"Christine," Johnny said firmly, and her eyelids fluttered.

"She's been breathing the whole time," Cole told him.

"Good."

Mitch, still in his armchair, had sat up to watch.

Gordon the Accident sprawled at the end of the couch. He was even paler than the girl. His forehead had a sheen of sweat on it.

This place could seduce anyone into sloppiness, Cole felt. It was no place for a new heme to be allowed to indulge himself without supervision. "Sandor should be here," he told Johnny. "This is his responsibility."

"He'll be back soon," Johnny said. "She *is* all right. She's not in shock; she's just fainted. Seth, if you carry her, we'll put her in the back bedroom. Then if you bring some juice from the kitchen, we'll see if we can perk her up a bit. Cole, can you take care of Gordon?"

Cole eyed Gordon the Accident, whose eyes were shut, head lolling on the back of the couch, hands limp beside him.

Can I? Yes. Do I want to? No. That sudden flash of memory had made him uncomfortable; it had felt like a warning signal, even though it had disappeared in an instant.

But all he said was "Yes." Feelings were no basis for judgment. He himself hadn't overindulged in a very long time. But he remembered how it felt, and he knew what to do.

"Gordon," he said, firm and clear, "I'm Cole. Can you stand up?"

Gordon didn't answer, but his eyes opened. In them Cole read surprise, confusion, and more than a little alarm.

"Come on," Cole told him. "Time to go to the bathroom."

The boy didn't move.

Cole took him by the arm and tried to pull him to sit up. It was like tugging at a sack of wet sand. "Get up!" he said sharply, his discomfort sliding into annoyance. "Don't be a baby."

At that Gordon feebly let Cole hoist him to his feet. He listed so heavily that Cole had to tug one of Gordon's arms over his own shoulder to keep the boy up.

Together, they trudged to the bathroom.

Cole maneuvered Gordon close to the toilet, then unloaded him onto the floor. He opened the lid and stood back. "Stick your finger down your throat."

Gordon shook his head, miserable.

"It'll make you feel better," Cole explained, leaning against the sink. "You can lie around and be bloated, sick, vulnerable, and useless for the rest of the night, or you can take charge of yourself this moment."

Gordon's eyes had been closed, but now they opened just a slit. He didn't look at Cole, so whether he was feeling exhaustion, nausea, or hatred, Cole couldn't say.

It didn't really matter anyway. "Just do it," Cole said impatiently.

Gordon leaned over the toilet and obeyed.

Cole kept his head turned away. He thought about the cabdriver whose upholstery he had ruined. He was starting to feel a little sick himself.

Gordon, once started, didn't seem able to stop. "Shut your eyes," Cole ordered without looking. "Don't look down."

Soon after that everything grew quiet. Gordon flushed the toilet, and Cole handed him a dampened towel to wipe his face with.

"God," Gordon said, draped exhaustedly over the toilet, "I just want to go home."

"Don't worry, I'll get you there. Where are you staying? Here with Johnny, or in one of the apartments?"

"I want to go to my *real* home."

His real home? Hadn't Sandor told this boy how things were? That he could never go home again? That he was cut off from his former life just as surely as if he were a newborn whose umbilical cord had been severed?

If not, Cole ought to tell him.

"You've got to feed now," he said instead. Better to stick to practical matters—let Sandor handle the messy emotional nuances of the kid's upheaval.

Number one problem: The kid was now empty, and soon Thirst would begin to thread its way through his body. He needed to feed quickly—not much, just enough to prevent need.

But Gordon sat there unmoving, evidently still nauseated. So Cole slipped out quietly, shutting the bathroom door behind him. Within a minute he was back with one of the omnis from the living room in tow. "Sit up," he told Gordon.

Gordon groaned.

"You don't have to take much," Cole said, "just a bit. Everything will be all right once you get back in balance."

"I can't."

"Yes, you can. You have to."

Gordon opened his eyes and saw the omni boy. Cole noted the way his gaze went eagerly to the boy's neck, darting over the exposed bits of skin. Yes. Now instinct would take over.

But Gordon shook his head. "That's a *dude*," he said from the floor.

"What?"

"No way I'm putting my lips on a *guy*."

Cole stared at him blankly. Incredible—this kid was incredible.

Where was Sandor? Sandor was the one who should be dealing with this.

Cole kept a grip on his temper. "Look at it this way," he told Gordon, letting his voice flow, calm and sensible. "Until recently you ate meat, right? Hamburgers, steak? But you never cared whether it came from a cow or a steer."

32

"I never had to put my mouth on a steer's *neck*."

"Gordon." Cole kept his voice firm. "Look at me."

Gordon focused on him.

"Take some now, or you may kill someone later. Is that what you want?"

That got through, a little. Gordon blinked, and doubt began to creep over his face.

Cole gave the omni boy a look, and the boy knelt beside Gordon. He held his hand out, palm up, with a little smirk that did not go unnoticed by Cole.

"Gordon," Cole repeated.

Slowly, Gordon pushed himself to sit up.

"Here, let me." Cole took the boy's hand and, leaning over it, fished inside his shirt for his cross. He pulled it out and pricked the wrist. Then he offered the wrist to Gordon.

Gordon did not look at Cole, or the boy. But he took the hand between his thumb and forefinger and gingerly lifted it to his mouth with an expression of distaste, which disappeared as he began sucking cautiously.

Cole looked away, down at the tile floor. "The veins flow more steadily than arteries," he said into the silence. "They contain less oxygen but are easier to control. That makes it easier to control yourself. And self-control, *Gordon*," he added, pausing for emphasis, "is the key to *everything*."

He waited a few more moments, gauging the time, then said, "That's enough," and reached over to pull the wrist away. But he held it just a second longer, to make the omni boy look up at him, so he could see Cole's cold stare warning him that he'd better not smirk again.

The boy saw. He seemed to wilt a little.

Then Cole released the wrist. "Thank you," he said, a cool dismissal.

The boy left without a word. And rapidly.

Gordon did not thank Cole. He did not say anything, just sat there, slumped and dejected. Cole watched him, thinking what to say next.

"It's done," he told Gordon abruptly. "You've learned something. And now you must get up."

Gordon shook his head but obeyed, getting to his feet. He was slightly taller than Cole, but his eyes were big and sad—yes, like a puppy's.

"How old are you?" Cole asked him.

"Eighteen."

Cole put one hand on the boy's shoulder—not out of companionship but to guide him back into the heart of the Colony.

"I really want to wake up now," Gordon said, his lip trembling—and Cole saw, to his horror, that the downcast eyes appeared to be brimming with tears.

But there was nothing he could say to make it better. "I know you do," he said, his voice flat, and he did not look again. Pity would help no one, and getting sucked into an emotional response would be one step toward the brink of a long slippery slope. He knew that from experience.

CHAPTER FOUR

THE living room looked as it had when Cole had first come in. Johnny had taken the omni girl off somewhere. Mitch was still in his chair. The two remaining omnis were lazing again. Cole knew that if he got closer to the back door he'd still be able to hear Frederick droning on. Frederick *always* droned on. And except for the occasional feed, Cole knew, Frederick hadn't left the Building in well over a hundred years.

This place is soft, Cole thought. An incompetent new heme walking around, and no one saw the need to keep an eye on him. Apparently nobody had even bothered to teach him the basics of feeding. Cole doubted anyone would do much more than bat an eye when they found out what had just happened.

Still, it wasn't Cole's job to babysit.

Gordon hadn't moved to sit down. He just stood in the middle of the living room looking overwhelmed, and rather lost.

As Cole watched, he sniffed and swiped his eyes with his sleeve.

"When Sandor comes," Cole said to Mitch, "tell him we're in the kitchen." Mitch waved that he'd heard. And Cole guided Gordon through the swinging door.

The kitchen was empty. If Seth had gotten juice for the girl, he was long gone. A faint odor of recently baked bread permeated the air. Not fresh—whatever cooking had been done had taken place several days ago. The kitchen was mostly for the omnis, who were not allowed to bring food out into the rest of the apartment, and it was an inviting place—or would have been if it wasn't for the warm yeasty-wheat smell, which was stomach turning to Cole. Its brick floors and granite countertops had been designed with two things in mind: preventing fires and keeping the omnis happy. The large table in the nook at the end had a cast-iron frame and a tiled top. In the middle stood a stainless steel container filled with yellow roses. *Real roses*, Cole noticed, catching the faint, soft scent.

Gordon slouched wearily into the chair Cole pulled out for him. Cole took a seat opposite.

They waited in silence. Gordon did not move. Cole sat, elbows on the table, his fingers laced, observing Gordon. Now that the boy wasn't feeding or puking, Cole could see the shocked, slightly bewildered look in his red-rimmed eyes—the same one Cole had seen in omnis as they walked away after having survived a car accident.

He felt another stir of sympathy but pushed it away. Anger, on the other hand—now *that* was called for. The Building hemes had obviously let the kid feed as freely as he had wanted on the resident omnis, without rules, without any attempt at discipline, without giving him any concept of moderation or restraint. The Colony hemes weren't lazy; he knew they all did their share—more than their share—of running the Colony. And he knew that most of them—no, all of them except Frederick—tried to feed mostly outside the Building. But their feeds were more like grazing, contentedly and easily like cattle, and if the grazing seemed as though it might get difficult, they came here rather than sort through the difficulties. It probably hadn't occurred to

them that a new heme would need structure and guidance.

Sandor—Sandor, who was responsible for the kid—
was soft in different ways. He lived on the road, like
Cole, and was sharp in that respect. But he had a
heart like a marshmallow. And he had not done right
by this boy.

Cole gave the pale face a silent appraisal. The kid
was very young. Physically, about the age Cole had been
when Johnny had created *him*.

But mentally, emotionally? Worse than a child. He
couldn't even care for himself.

What *had* Sandor been doing for him?

Now Cole took his time reading the clues on Gordon's
face. There was a haggard look about him, and the
deep-set eyes—which were hazel, damn it, not black,
not like Guerdon's at all, so why did they give Cole the
feeling he already knew this kid?—had dark circles
under them. The kid had not been sleeping well.

I just want to go home, he'd said. He was unhappy.
Having trouble adjusting.

"Would you like a glass of water?" Cole asked, making an effort to be kind.

39

Gordon didn't even bother to look up. "Do I *drink* water?" It was the nonresponse of a sullen teenager.

Cole was relieved; kindness apparently wasn't called for. "Every living thing needs water," he said, his voice curt now. "Are you a living thing?"

"You tell me."

"The answer is *yes*. Yes, you are a living thing, and therefore you do drink water. Weren't you sweating just now? Don't you urinate?"

"Yeah. But it's *blue*," Gordon said, angry.

Lashing out, Cole thought. *Because he doesn't like the situation he finds himself in.* It was useless behavior at best. Also rude—and very omni-like, in Cole's opinion.

"Some advice," he told Gordon. "Some *good* advice, and if you're wise, you'll take it: Don't dwell too much on your feelings just now. It will help you get used to things."

"I'm not going to get used to blue pee."

"Believe me, you will."

For answer, Gordon put his head in his hands. They sat there for a moment. Finally, Gordon said in a muffled voice, "I didn't mean to hurt her."

40

Self-pity. The boy probably had been wallowing in it for some time. He'd been indulged and pampered, when what he'd needed was a heme boot camp.

"There's no room for 'mean to' in the life of a heme," Cole told him.

"I don't understand this place," Gordon said into his hands. "I don't understand what I'm supposed to do. She said to take her to the edge. Isn't that what she meant?"

"You went *past* the edge."

Gordon lifted his head, but he wouldn't look at Cole. His face and body proclaimed that he was still immersed in his own misery. "I thought since I wasn't hungry—"

"You don't get *hungry*," Cole said coldly. "*Nobody* gets hungry. We feel *Thirst*—and you shouldn't even feel *that* if you conduct yourself with any sense at all. In any case, you are not an omni anymore, so stop talking like one. And we're all very lucky you *weren't* feeling Thirst, because you would have killed her."

"But I kept my hands off her. I thought—"

"That was the only smart thing you did. If you'd been holding her, she wouldn't have fallen like that; and none of us would have known anything was wrong until

41

it was too late. So you can feel fortunate you did exactly one thing right."

At that moment Sandor came in, holding the swinging door carefully so it made no noise.

Sandor was powerfully built. He looked like someone who had been in a lot of brawls, but Cole knew that his crooked nose came from a girl throwing a flowerpot at him in a fit of jealousy. It had healed before it could be reset, and Sandor would not consent to have it broken again so that it could be straightened.

"Cole!" He came to wrap Cole up in a bear hug.

"Hello, Sandor," Cole said, his voice muffled against the genial shoulder, which was covered in a thick, shapeless sweater. Sandor might be sturdy, but he always seemed to be cold. He'd shaved off that rust-colored beard he'd had last time Cole had seen him.

"So, little fellow," Sandor said, peering closely at Gordon as he drew up a chair. "I hear you had a difficulty while I was gone."

"A difficulty." Cole snorted. "Just a small one. Haven't you taught him *anything*?"

"Teaching takes time, Cole," Sandor said, calm. "But I can see why you're worried."

"I'm not worried."

"Of course you are. I've known you for more than a hundred and eighty years, and I say you're quite perturbed. But to answer your question," he continued as Cole tried to speak, "Gordon can't learn everything all at once. That's why I brought him here, so he could start off in a protected environment."

"I'm not sure having omnis at his beck and call is a good way to start off."

"But don't you think it's better to start off gently, ease him into it? You see my point, do you not?"

Cole *did* see his point; Cole had once tried to make the transition gradual and easy.

"No," he told Sandor.

Then he turned to Gordon. "Listen here," he said, making his voice sharp, so the kid would pay attention. "This is important. You do not have the experience to combine any kind of sexual contact with the feed. Keep the two completely separate until someone—like Sandor—tells you that you are ready to do otherwise. That means no touching, no kissing, and certainly no rubbing up against people."

"How can I feed if I don't touch anybody?"

"Maybe if you only feed from *dudes* for a while, you'll learn where the line is drawn."

"Now, Cole," Sandor said, "don't you think you're being a little hard on the boy? It's only been a couple of weeks—"

"In a couple of weeks he can create a dozen more fools just like him. What *have* you taught him, Sandor? What does he know?"

Sandor sighed. "Go on," he told Gordon. "Tell him some of the things you've learned."

Gordon didn't reply. He glared down at the tiled tabletop.

"Go on," Sandor urged.

"We drink blood," Gordon intoned.

"No kidding," said Cole. "What else?"

"We can't go out in sunlight."

"Why not?"

"Because we blister."

"'Blister,'" Cole echoed, and for once he didn't bother to keep the bitterness out of his voice. "What a funny little word. What does it mean, Gordon?"

"It means. . . . I don't know. Sunlight hurts us."

Cole cast a quick piercing glance at Sandor. "Let me describe what it means," he told Gordon.

44

"Oh, Cole, no," Sandor said sadly.

"Your skin burns and falls off—just the skin at first, which exposes the nerves. And then if you don't get to safety, your insides start cooking."

"Really, Cole," Sandor said, shaking his head, "you're going to scare him."

"He needs to be scared. He has no caution. He has no control. Gordon, listen to this. Our bodies heal." Cole hesitated, then pressed on. "Our minds don't. And in sun, your mind goes too, before the end." Of course Gordon didn't notice the effort it took to say that, and if Sandor did, he knew better than to show it. "But even when it's all gone, when all that's left of you is just a heap of charred bone and tattered flesh, you're still alive. Do you understand? There must be hundreds, maybe thousands of us who were thought to be dead, all under the ground, conscious but inert, staring at a coffin lid only inches away, in the dark."

He felt immensely satisfied, because the sulky expression on Gordon's face was gone, replaced by horrified fascination.

With a touch of doubt, Cole noticed. Hmm. *That* wasn't good.

"Well," said Sandor, shifting in his chair. "That's

enough to give anyone nightmares for a decade or so."

"Good. I hope Gordon is now afraid to even blink until he's asked you whether it's a good idea." Cole turned back to Gordon. "In what ways can we die?"

Gordon shook his head.

"You don't know? Any theories?"

"I don't know," Gordon said.

"That's right; you don't. Because, guess what, Gordon, we *can't* die."

"Now, Cole," Sandor put in, "you don't know that."

"When have you seen anyone die, Sandor?"

"I don't like to bring up an old argument, but Harold died."

Cole sat back in his chair. It *was* an old argument, and neither of them ever budged on it. "He did not."

"I think he did. It's a matter of debate," Sandor told Gordon, who had forgotten his self-pity for the moment and was paying full attention. "There were a few of us who crashed an omni party at a park, and the omnis had brought dirt bikes. Some of us took turns riding them, and Harold unfortunately rode into a low-strung cable. It took his head right off. Oh, the omnis screamed."

"Everyone screamed," Cole said.

"Yes. But," Sandor added quickly, "I feel fairly sure that he died."

"No. When his head was lying there in the grass, his eyes moved," Cole said.

"Cole does not lie," Sandor told Gordon. "But what he saw, in the eyes, I didn't see."

"They moved," Cole said.

"You imagined it. You know his muscles were use-less—how could he move his eyes?"

"They did move."

"So you say. I think you were too upset to observe as dispassionately as you would like to think. One moment Harold was speeding by as he demonstrated the rebel yell," Sandor told Gordon, "and the next his head was flying through the air while his body kept riding the dirt bike. It was quite horrible to see. Emotions were high."

"What . . . what happened to the . . . body?" Gordon asked. "If there was a question about whether he was really . . . you know."

"Buried," Cole said. "Even we can't grow new heads."

"There," Sandor said cheerfully. "That's one thing Cole and I agree on. We cannot grow new heads. It is

47

true, Gordon, that our bodies go into a sort of hibernation if we go too long without sustenance. This sleep looks like death, but it is not. So you must be sure to feed often, and regularly."

"And don't forget," Cole said. "Long before hibernation comes the Thirst, which turns you into an animal—all instinct, no control. The point being," he added, "that everything you do now has consequences, Gordon. You can't ignore them. You can't get away from them. You can't get away from *anything*. Like"—he looked around the kitchen, casting about for an example, and landed on the roses—"spring. People always look forward to spring, don't they? Everything comes to life—but it's just going to die again. Everything starts anew in the spring—but the clock is ticking on all that newness; it is always ticking on every bit of life—except you. You get to watch the clock tick. You get to watch everyone you've ever loved die and leave you. You get to watch everything you've ever known change and disappear."

"You are so depressing, Cole," Sandor burst out. "You would try the patience of a saint with your 'We cannot die' and 'The clock is ticking.'"

"You're not doing Gordon any service by letting him

think that he can treat this lightly."

"He has plenty of time to learn how to treat it," Sandor said easily. "As do we all."

Cole suddenly realized how tired he was. He looked at his watch: past four thirty in the morning. The Building was safe from sunlight; he could keep any hours he liked here. But he was used to being safely in bed well before dawn.

"Did you see Johnny when you came in?" he asked Sandor.

"No. They said he was in the back bedroom, tending to—what was her name? Carol?"

"Christine."

Gordon showed no interest in Christine, or in anything else now. Cole watched his eyes. His head was bowed, but his eyes flicked back and forth, locking on nothing; he was thinking.

About what?

It was hard to tell now. There was obviously a lot going through his head. His eyes darted up once, across and past Cole's. That was a sign of his newness, too. Omnis, unless they wanted sex, had trouble meeting people's gazes for long. The rest of the time they were like dogs, for whom eye contact implied social dominance.

Cole thought of the flash of memory that had come earlier. It was completely gone now. There was nothing here, he told himself, that had any connection to his long-dead brother.

"Well!" Sandor said, slapping his hands on the arms of his chair. "We could have wished for a more uplifting conversation, could we not?" he asked Gordon cheerfully. "But here's something positive to take from it: You can always count on Cole to tell you the truth. He is one of the most honest people you will ever meet, and the most trustworthy."

"I lie to omnis all the time," Cole pointed out.

"You see? Even to his own detriment, he must tell the truth. Ah, I'm glad to be in your company again, Cole—it's just like old times. And this evening has ended without disaster, so all is well. It's turned out to be a fine night!"

A fine night indeed, Cole thought. He had to admit now that he would not see Johnny again tonight. Johnny would stay by that girl's side until she was not only conscious, but alert.

He rose, pushing his chair back. "I'm going to turn in."

"We will talk more tomorrow night," Sandor said. Cole gave him a brief nod.

Gordon was still deep in thought, his brow furrowed. He did not seem to hear either of them, nor to notice when Cole walked out.

The living room was empty now. Some of the others were still outside, though—as Cole walked past he could hear their voices through the open door, rising and falling, washing into the living room in murmured waves.

He didn't even pause. He wasn't in the mood to chat right now, and there would be plenty of time tomorrow night to see everyone. After all, he hadn't come here to socialize.

As to just exactly why he *had* come—well, it looked as if he'd have to wait another evening to find out.

CHAPTER FIVE

EARLY the next evening Cole got his laundry started in the basement before heading back up to Johnny's.

He wondered whether it might be best to feed here in the Building again, to save time. There was no telling how long a discussion he was in for tonight.

When he walked into the living room, Sandor was sitting on the sofa talking to Mina and Nell. They all turned at the sound of the door, and the room seemed to erupt in welcome.

"Cole!"

"There you are!"

He was a little taken aback—Mina and Nell had actually risen to greet him. He was used to not being noticed unless he *intended* to be noticed.

"Good evening," Sandor said. "Did you sleep well?"

"About like I usually do here."

"What a welcome you had last night," Mina said as she gave him a hug. "Sandor was telling us what happened."

"You didn't even come out to say hello." Nell hugged him in turn. "Shame on you."

"Sorry. I was tired."

Not only was he being noticed, he was being noticed for *himself*. He was used to pulling omnis in with his smile and his gaze. Omnis were all surface, and he'd lived among them for so long that he felt oddly naked to be looked at with such familiarity. It made him feel as if his flaws and his past were tattooed on his face.

"Is Johnny around yet?" he asked, nodding toward the patio.

"No," said Sandor, "he is slaving away in the office, as usual. I just left him pawing through about a million envelopes from Merrill Lynch."

Cole wasn't surprised. Johnny usually worked on business in late afternoon and early evening, rising while the sun was still up so he could make phone calls before the omnis' working day ended.

Mina and Nell sat down again. Cole lowered himself onto the broad arm of one of the overstuffed chairs.

"It *is* good to see you, Cole," Nell said. "How have you been?"

"Good." Cole liked Nell; she was frank and matter-of-fact. The only thing she seemed to change about herself over the years was the style of her glasses. He remembered the thick horn-rims, which had given way to big buglike plastic frames, which turned to wire rims, and which now seemed to be a sort of tortoiseshell.

"Traveled out of the country?" Mina asked.

"Not lately. I was in Toronto back in the midnineties, but that's about it." Cole turned to ask Sandor how Gordon had come about, how the change had happened, but Mina continued.

"Toronto's beautiful in the summer. I'm assuming you went in summer—as I recall, you don't like snow."

"Not much, no. You're right—I left when it started getting cold." He waited a moment, but she seemed to have finished that line of conversation and he turned back to Sandor. "So, how did it happen?"

"How did what—oh. That."

"Yes, that."

54

Sandor shook his head. "It was most regrettable."

"But what *happened*?"

"Ah." Sandor looked embarrassed. "Well, you know. Long story."

"I'd like to hear," Cole told him, although he knew he'd have to keep reining Sandor in and calling him back to the subject in order to get the story out. Sandor loved to talk.

"Well," he began, "I was in Missouri, of all places. It should have been nothing out of the ordinary. I was at one of the colleges, you know."

"So what went wrong?" Cole asked. He preferred college campuses himself. They had well-fed students wandering around at all hours and populations that changed constantly. "Were you in the dorms?"

"No, no, nothing like that. I was just getting settled in. I had checked into one of those cut-rate hotels—you know, the places where the relatives come to stay for football games and such. Look at you, so serious, trying to see where I made my mistake. But I tell you, it was just bad luck."

"You had checked in . . . ," Cole prodded.

"Yes. I put my bag in the room, and then I walked to

55

a bar across the street from the college. It was a sad day when they raised the drinking age, my friend. There was a time when a bar near a campus was full of drunken kids. Now, half of them drop out or graduate before they have even a chance to get shit faced in a public place." Sandor shook his head, sorry for the unwillingly sober teenagers of America.

"Go on."

"But you know me. Charming fellow that I am, I managed to get enough to hold me for a night or two. So I was feeling good and had time on my hands, and since it was early, I thought I would look around and see how the campus was laid out."

Cole nodded. Again, this was what he would have done.

"The hotel was across a small park from the main campus. The usual sort of thing—a playground, a creek, trees. And on the other side of the park, the college. It was a good night to be outside—sometimes I don't understand why the omnis don't roam at night. They always hurry like little insects from their cars to the store to the bar to the apartment, little bugs scurrying for shelter. Don't they ever take time to look up at the stars, to wonder?"

"They're afraid, Sandor. Go on with your story."

"Ah, yes. I went into the park, and there was a path that led down to the creek, to a small bridge that crossed it. And from there, up to the parking lot by the dorms and the English building and so on. I walked around the campus and looked at the place. They had very nice fountains. One by the architecture building was especially nice; it looked like a pyramid with waterfalls—"

"And that's where things went wrong?"

"Oh no, it was just a nice fountain. I like the sound of running water. No, where things went wrong was when I started back to the hotel, when I got to the parking lot and left the sidewalk to go down into the little woods to cross the bridge. It was such a small woods; what harm could come to anyone there? Even a rabbit or a mouse wouldn't have felt—all right, I see you don't care for my thoughts on these matters, so I will try to stick to the facts.

"As I was walking down the path to the small bridge, I heard footsteps behind me, and I turned to see who it was, and it was a teenage boy. And I said to myself, 'Why Sandor, God has placed this beautiful boy for you to have a little treat; why not take a small sip and enjoy the night a little longer?' So I slowed my pace to let him catch up with me, which he did, just as I stepped off the footbridge.

"Let me tell you, I was smiling. I smelled the wet earth beneath us and heard the wind in the trees above us, and I was about to have a taste of young boy to round off the pleasant evening, then perhaps go back and watch a bit of television before having a nice restful sleep. I was listening to his footsteps on the bridge, and I thought he was about to try to pass me.

"But he didn't. 'Don't turn around,' I heard him say. And at the same moment I felt something sharp prod me in the back, something exactly like . . . a knife."

Sandor looked around at his audience, drawing out the moment.

"I laughed, I tell you. A knife! The hunted hunting the hunter! It was too amusing. I thought, 'Will *he* be surprised before this night is through! Yes, this will teach him not to go poking people with knives, the silly boy.'

"So I played along, I did as he asked and did not turn around, and I tried very hard not to laugh. And I did *not* laugh—until he ordered me to give him my wallet. Then of course I could not help but give a small chuckle. That made him angry, I think, because he cut me with the knife a bit, just in the small of my back, a tiny jab to frighten me; and I laughed even more as I told him, 'I'll not give you a thing, little fellow.' And do you know what he did then?"

The living room was quiet, as all three of them listened. Cole knew he must be the only one who had not heard this before, but Sandor was quite the storyteller, and he enjoyed holding them all in the palm of his hand.

"He stabbed me," Sandor said. "Right between the ribs. The blade slid into my back as if it had been greased. Now, my friend, I have not been stabbed in a long time, and I hope not to be again for many years more, because it hurts like the devil, let me tell you. Of course, because of the pain I was surprised, and while I was surprised that little shit grabbed my hair and pulled my head back and slit my throat.

"Now, I ask you, is that any way to behave? Trying to kill someone just because they don't want to give you their wallet? I don't know what the world is coming to."

"So this boy was Gordon?" Cole asked. He thought: *Wonderful; we have a conscienceless killer among us.*

"I'm coming to that. Now the wound in my back had already healed of course; as soon as he jerked the blade out I could feel the edges of flesh pull back together. But my throat! Have you ever had your throat cut, Cole?"

"No, Sandor, I have not."

"Let me tell you, it is like a suitcase being unzipped. Not only does it hurt as badly as being stabbed, but everything pours out so quickly that you lose large quantities of blood even before the wound heals. I've never felt anything like it. I remember I put my hands up, without thinking, trying to hold it all in. It was extraordinary. He halfway took my head off. My windpipe was cut, and I could not speak, only gurgle, and even that only down in my chest. I actually got dizzy— dizzy! Woozy, like when I was a boy and we used to take turns rolling down the hill in a barrel. I did not fall, but I staggered, and do you know what that boy was doing all this time?"

"What?"

"He was rummaging my pockets. He was quite focused on his mission, I must say that for him. I was wearing my overcoat, you know, because it was chilly, and he was going through my pockets—ah, don't look at me like that, Cole; you know what they say: Cold hands, warm heart."

"I was just thinking that if this was May in Missouri, you must have looked rather out of place in your overcoat. If the police had found you lurking in the woods, they might have thought you were a flasher."

"Maybe that's where the police were, out looking for flashers, because they certainly weren't looking for murdering robbers too young to even shave! That boy should have been home playing his video games, not out cutting honest men's throats."

"But go on, Sandor."

"Yes. Well, he took what he wanted, and then he pushed me. I staggered a bit, you see, and he pushed me—and I lost my footing and fell. I rolled and slid down the side of the ravine, while that little shit got away with my wallet. I had to get Johnny to send a new driver's license, and I had to call and cancel the credit cards! Did you know you have to pay for the first fifty dollars of whatever they steal? It's a terrible cheat if you ask me."

"Did you chase after Gordon?"

"I did not say that was Gordon. You're getting ahead of the story. So I was lying there on my back, listening to his footsteps as he ran away, and I was looking up at the stars through the branches. They look like lace, you know—branches—and in the city the stars look faded— the ones that you can see. They must be quite deter- mined to be seen at all, the stars in the city."

"Sandor."

"Sorry, sorry. Anyway, I was drained. Almost com- pletely drained. Have you ever been drained, Cole?"

"No. Not after the first time."

"Well, I was. Perhaps you remember how your heart pounds and how your head clears to make you an ani- mal, with animal sharpness. The air becomes so clear, every sound distinct and separate. Do you remember that, Cole?"

"Yes." Of course he did. They all did.

"Then also you remember how the Thirst drives you, how you can smell blood and flesh on the breeze, how you can hear the pulse of other beings, because all there is in the world is their blood and your emptied veins and your empty stomach and your empty mouth."

Cole nodded. He remembered—but he didn't like to.

It was something he lived to avoid.

"My throat had healed, but I was empty, and in this state I smelled an omni before I heard him. He smelled of alcohol, and laundry detergent, and cigarette smoke, and leather.

"And then—you know. I was on my feet and moving, low to the ground. I could not help it. You know how one cannot control oneself at times like that."

"Yes, I know. So *that* was Gordon?"

"Yes. The poor fellow was drunk. He was coming down to cross the bridge but was too inebriated to walk properly. Just before I took him down, he collapsed—his knees folded right up, and together we tumbled down the bank next to the bridge. I remember he was holding beer cans, because they fell with us, and as I fed they were spewing into the dirt."

"Wrong place at the wrong time."

"Oh yes. Poor fellow. But I look at it this way; at least we don't have a thieving murderer in our midst, because that's who I would have gotten to first if Gordon hadn't shown up at that very moment."

"Instead we have a drunken frat boy."

"Now, be fair, Cole; he's not drunk now and never will

be again. Poor boy, I was completely wild. It was . . . regrettable."

Sandor's voice was low now. There was a lot he was not saying, and didn't have to say. Everyone knew it, because everyone had felt it at least once, although not to the death as Sandor had.

Feeding to fill emptiness—it was glorious, it was gluttony, it was madness—and once begun, a heme could not stop.

Mina and Nell were silent, perhaps thinking of their own first times.

Cole wondered how Sandor had handled the problems that must have immediately arisen with Gordon, but before he could ask, someone came out of the little hallway next to the stairs.

Johnny was here.

CHAPTER SIX

"EVENING, Cole," said Johnny. "I see Sandor's been telling you his tale. Unfortunate, that."

"Yes," said Cole, standing up.

"I didn't get a chance to thank you for your help last night."

"How's the girl doing?"

"Christine," Johnny reminded him. "She's not happy about being barred from feeds for a while, but other than that she seems fine. I expect she's outside. Shall we head that way?"

As they approached the glass door, Cole saw that Frederick was in the same seat he'd been in last night. This time an omni was seated on a stool at his feet, looking up at him with an expression of adoration, as if Frederick were a god. He held the girl's hand in his as he spoke, playing absently with her fingers. Frederick had always reveled in the devotion of his omnis, whom he kept like pets.

Johnny slid the door open and stood back, letting the others go first.

"Cole!" Elise stood up to greet him.

"Lo, the prodigal has returned," Frederick said. He did *not* stand up.

"It's been too long," said Alice, nodding. She didn't get up either, but her lap was full of papers.

The omnis quietly watched the hemes greet each other. Besides Frederick's pet omni, Mary Kate was there, her eyes intent on Cole. There was a man in a black leather duster wearing black-and-silver boots up to the knees. Christine, the girl from last night, still looked a little pale—but otherwise healthy—and tonight she wore nipple rings connected by chains apparent through the light gauze of her dress. A scrawny owl-eyed kid in a black cape had drawn an ankh on his cheek. They were glaringly, obviously omni; hemes could not afford to make fashion statements.

Johnny still stood by the open door. "Christine, Kendra, Boris, Mary Kate, and Shayne—"

"Osiris," corrected the kid in the cape.

"Yes, sorry—Osiris. Would you all mind stepping into the house for a bit?"

As they reluctantly began to obey, Cole saw that there was one omni Johnny had not mentioned, sitting in the shadows in a corner next to the wall. She was so old that her skin appeared to have shrunken onto her skull and her head wobbled, but Cole recognized her. Helene, who had been quite wrinkled the last time Cole had been here; she was still alive, amazingly enough.

That was Johnny all over. Johnny did not get rid of his omnis, not as long as they wanted to stay. They could be in diapers or bedridden and still Johnny would keep them. And when they finally died, he would pay for the funeral and the headstone. Johnny was ruthless when he had to be, Cole knew—but he could also be tenderhearted.

Right now Johnny was still at the door. He had stopped Christine to ask how she was, so Cole made his way around the chairs and squatted in front of Helene.

Her skin hung from her bones like powdery spiderwebs, soft and white from all the years away from sunlight. "Helene," he said, "do you remember me? Cole?"

Helene's eyes latched onto him. "Of course I do," she said firmly, but there was no spark of recognition, and her eyes were uncertain. "Do you want to feed?"

He looked down at her hand on the arm of the chair and saw that the skin over the knotted blue veins was thinner than paper. He patted it and said, "It's good to see you. How are you feeling?"

"Not good," Helene said fretfully. "I joined the army, you see, but they aren't giving me my money, and I have to pay rent or they're going to put me out."

"No one's going to put you out," Cole said. "This is your home."

"But I don't have any *money*." Her voice scaled up, urgent.

"You don't need to worry about money, Helene," Sandor said, pulling up a chair for himself. "Remember? Johnny's taking care of everything."

Helene sat forward suddenly, eyes focused on Sandor, sharp as a bird's. "Would *you* like to feed?"

"Not right now," Sandor said calmly. "But I thank you."

She looked at Cole and opened her mouth—but he shook his head no.

Her eyes went vague again, and she settled back in her chair.

"So, has the aesthete yet indulged himself?" Frederick asked Cole as Cole got up and took a seat next to Nell.

"He did last night," Mitch said helpfully before Cole could answer.

"How enjoyable. I refuse to go on the road," Frederick announced to no one in particular. "I'm much too greedy. I could never deny myself for more than a few hours."

"Nell," Johnny said from the doorway, "would you help Helene to get inside?"

Cole saw that the other omnis were gone. Now there wasn't a single item of clothing that would have drawn a second glance in a mall, on a campus, or on any suburban street.

Nell eased Helene to her feet, and the two slowly made their way inside. Cole looked around at all the familiar faces. So far it wasn't much of a meeting; he and Sandor were the only ones who didn't keep their territory close to the Building.

"Is anyone else coming?" he asked.

"No," Johnny said. "You were the only one I called in."

"Ah." Cole nodded, but he was suddenly uncomfortable. He scrutinized Johnny's face—it showed nothing, of course. "Then why am *I* here?" he asked.

"In a word," Johnny said, "Gordon."

"Gordon?"

"Yes. The lad's been with us a fortnight," said Johnny. "We've been talking, Cole. We've agreed that Sandor should take Gordon on the road for a few months and begin teaching him how to get along outside the Building."

"I couldn't agree more," Cole told him.

"So far he's only been exposed to what amounts to a teenage boy's picnic." That was Mina. "All he's been doing is lying around, feeding, and having sex. He needs to start seeing some of our responsibilities."

Cole nodded. He noticed that everyone was looking at him. "It sounds reasonable to me," he said out loud. "More than reasonable. It's necessary."

"I'm glad you think so," Johnny said. "Because we feel that you should go with them."

CHAPTER SEVEN

IT took a moment to sink in.

"Did you say—*me?*" Cole asked, shifting in his chair.

"Yes." Johnny eyed him calmly. "You and Sandor would make a well-rounded team."

"*Please* take the Accident out of here," said Frederick. "He's practically an omni."

"But . . . *me?*" Cole asked.

Sandor chuckled. "We've been round on this subject already, Cole. It has been agreed that the boy may benefit from a firmer hand than mine from time to time."

But that wasn't what Cole had meant. "I—I do *not* have a . . . good track record with this sort of thing," he reminded them.

"That was an entirely different situation," Johnny said, "and it was long ago. You've become very controlled.

Cautious. Observant. And extraordinarily conscientious. You do see this, don't you? And together, you and Sandor make one perfect teacher. He's a bit of an extrovert, which is good. He's impulsive, affectionate, softhearted. Wonderful qualities, but even he agrees they need some balance. Besides, we feel it's best that there be two of you keeping an eye on things. Consider it a safety net. The entire responsibility won't fall on you, lad. It will be shared."

"It's natural that you would view this through a certain emotional . . . curtain," Alice put in. "But look at it logically. You live outside the Building, outside the city, among omnis, in fact. Your experience is practical and deep." Her voice was placid, factual. "You have always adjusted quickly to changing situations. And I have to say, that whole unfortunate episode with Elizabeth—"

"Alice," said Johnny.

"He's the one who brought up his track record."

Nell opened her mouth to say something but seemed to change her mind.

"All I was going to say," Alice continued mildly, "was that what Elizabeth did was not in his control. If he thinks it was, he's being ridiculous. Really, Cole. I knew you were upset at the time, but I thought you'd have gained some perspective by now."

Cole shook his head, unable to think of anything to say. He was the only one of the whole group who *had* perspective. The only one who had failed on not one but two counts. The second failure was the one that was more pertinent now.

He had already shown himself to be inadequate in training a new heme.

It *had* been long ago—more than a hundred and twenty years. Of course, he'd been failing miserably for decades before that with his sympathetic, ineffectual attempts to help her become resigned to her new life. She'd rejected his kindness, his teaching, and finally his presence. But the defining, crystal clear culmination of his failure had taken place when she showed up in New York again, back when the Building was one of the new apartment houses scattered among the shanties and lots, bound by equally new grids of paved streets and sidewalks.

It was the pristine new sidewalk outside the Building that had broken her body. Everyone else had been sleeping in the afternoon hours when she'd climbed the ladder from the top floor to the roof. The hatch was heavy, and it must have thudded shut behind her when she stepped onto the roof—but Cole hadn't heard it. No one had. No one heard any cries when the sun pierced her skin, or when she jumped from the roof's edge. No one heard her body hit the pavement.

No one had known at all till the police came.

"Look around you, lad," Johnny was saying now. "Who has sharper skills? None of us, I'd say. You've been on the road for a century."

Johnny was the one who'd gotten her back. Cole had been nothing but a raving mess, burned in his own turn from trying to get out to the sidewalk. Cole hadn't been strong enough, had turned back on the stoop with his skin a sheet of pain, his eyes digging sharp wheels of flame into his brain. His sight had come back in a couple of hours, enough to see his skin as it healed. And while he was laid up, unable to move without agony, Johnny had taken care of everything that could be taken care of—the questioning authorities, the curious omnis—and had gotten her back from the morgue.

Cole didn't like to think what Johnny had risked—or what he had done—to accomplish all that.

"We've discussed it," Johnny was telling him. "Hands down, we think you're the best choice."

"You know," said Sandor, "we haven't even asked Gordon if he *wants* to go on the road."

"Who cares what he wants?" Frederick said. "Two weeks ago he was eating cooked animal flesh and downing six-packs. He'll do as he's told."

"What say you, Cole?" That was Johnny.

"I say . . ." As he hesitated, he happened to look up, and for the first time he saw the way that some of the hemes—Nell and Sandor in particular—were looking at him. With kindness and pity.

He suddenly realized that everyone could see his surprise, his hesitation. His doubt.

He drew a deep breath, and let his face relax till he was sure it showed nothing.

"I need to think," he said calmly. "Give me a few minutes."

Johnny nodded. There was a short silence, and then the others began to converse in low murmurs.

All right. He must be logical: The question at hand was not whether he had gained perspective or whether he'd once been upset. Dwelling on past mistakes served no purpose. He normally didn't even allow himself to think about them. Would not have now if he hadn't been taken by surprise.

The fact was, Gordon *did* need to go on the road. It was in the best interest of everyone here. *Someone* had to take him out and train him.

If Cole said no—if he shirked—the burden would fall to someone else. Who would be best for the job? Johnny, obviously—but it wouldn't be right for Johnny to leave all his other duties behind to work with this one boy.

What about the other hemes in the Building?

No candidates came to mind. Look at what had happened just in last night's small, easily contained emergency. Of the hemes who lived here in the Building, only Johnny had reacted quickly and with decision. Everyone else had seemed content to let someone else take care of it. Mitch had sat and watched from a distance. Seth had followed directions—*Cole's* directions.

And no one—out of all the hemes living in the Building—had yet bothered to supervise the kid. He'd been here for two weeks, and no one had tried to ease him into the difficulties and nuances of independent feeding.

Gordon had picked up bad habits. Who knew how deeply they were ingrained or how difficult it would be to rid him of them?

Cole looked around the group. "How well does Gordon listen?" he asked. "How obedient is he?" It was a simple question, but no one answered. "Sandor?"

"You saw him last night—he's moody, still in a bit of shock. I haven't wanted to push him too much."

So no one had any idea whether the kid would catch on quickly or have to have his lessons pounded home. No idea how difficult this might or might not be.

"Has Gordon fed tonight?" Cole asked.

"I don't believe so," Sandor said. "He's been low-spirited, poor boy, since last night. I left him lying on his bed watching game show reruns."

"Let's take him out."

"You mean outside the Building?"

"Yes."

"To feed?"

"Yes."

"Is this the beginning of his training, or is it a test to see whether you *want* to train him?"

"A test."

"Well, then, we'll hope he passes. There's a coffee bar on the corner—shall we try that?"

"Maybe not coffee bars just yet," Cole said. "We want the feeds to be a bit sluggish, not hopped up on caffeine."

"A bar then? Dance club?"

"Either's fine."

"Seth told me about a nice bar down Broadway," Sandor said, rising from his chair. "You and Gordon and I can go check it out."

"No," said Cole. "Let's you and I get ourselves taken care of first. That way there will be no distractions."

"Just feed here then," Frederick suggested.

Sandor shook his head. "I hate to see these poor omnis pale and drained all the time. Shall we go to Seth's bar, Cole?"

"You go ahead, Sandor. I need to finish a couple of chores here, and I'll catch a quick feed somewhere. Then we'll take Gordon out."

"As you wish." Sandor paused to pull the neck of his sweater up high around his ears, and then with a muffled "I'll be back shortly," he was gone.

Cole rose with a glance at Johnny: *I'll make a decision tonight.*

Johnny regarded him steadily. It was clear that he had already weighed the choices and was sure Cole was the best one.

Johnny's sureness was no small thing.

But as Cole slipped through the patio doorway into the apartment, he suddenly remembered how he'd failed to plan for the subway last night. Not a big deal, when it was just him.

However, slackness of that kind could be a very big deal if he had to deal with another person's safety as well as his own. Anything he let slide, anything he was lenient or careless about—any tiny particular could mean disaster, not only for the Accident, but for the Colony. If the boy Gordon got even a little bit out of control, he might draw the attention of omnis. Of police, of hospitals, of newspapers. Of mental institutions. Of funeral homes.

If Gordon got a *lot* out of control—but there was no point in thinking about that right now. No point in borrowing trouble.

First things first: He'd see how the kid did tonight.

Cole headed down into the basement; it was musty at the bottom of the wooden steps. The sides of the room were crowded with trunks, boxes, and artifacts left over from past wanderings of the New York City hemes.

When he'd come here earlier to start his laundry, he'd thought about digging around to see if he could find any of his old sketchbooks. Now he just wanted to finish the laundry and get going.

A single bare lightbulb hung in the center of the room, making a circle of light that dimmed before it reached the corners. He stood in the ring of light while he pulled his wet clothes out of the washing machine and loaded them into the dryer. A nice change, to have a dryer. A change from hanging things out in hotel rooms.

He did not want to take the kid on the road. He did not want traveling companions, even ones that *didn't* involve worry and care. Not that Sandor was so bad; Cole had traveled with Sandor before. It was just that Cole had grown used to being alone. And even if Gordon were an angel of a student—even if he were slavish about following directions and eager to learn— traveling with him meant that every word out of Cole's mouth would have to be some kind of direction, or correction, or advice.

He had just started the dryer when he heard someone coming downstairs from the first floor. He turned as a pair of black heeled shoes appeared and, rising up from them, bare legs. Next a short black skirt, then a black lacy top, and last of all black hair streaked purple and red in front.

At the bottom of the steps, Mary Kate hesitated. In that moment Cole suddenly blanked out on her name, so he just smiled a greeting—which was a mistake, because now she came over, slouching like some kind of cat into his cozy circle of light.

She stopped between him and the clothes dryer, so close that he could see her skin through the black lace of her blouse.

"I've been waiting for you," she said in a pouting voice as she leaned back against the dryer. Her eyes didn't leave his face. "I haven't let anybody else touch me since last night. I've saved it all for you. I thought we could combine."

Cole had never been on the omni end of combining sexual pleasure with the feed; but even after all these years he remembered how it felt to be fed on, even though there had been nothing sexual about it.

Those were the days when one *had* to go longer between feedings if one wasn't in a city. Now every heme took care to feed nightly, but Cole could remember a time when he left most of his feeds fainting, back when a meal came only a few times a week. Back when Johnny, too, was still a wanderer.

The way Johnny told it, one night he'd been arrested along with the drunks he was about to feed on after three nights of fasting. When the police then thought Johnny was attacking his fellow inmates, he'd been locked up alone in a dark jail cell. By the time they released him it was after sunrise, and he'd had to break into a nearby cellar, huddling there to painfully nurse his newly made burns and wait for night. Cole had been on his way home as the sun was going down on that fifth evening, just as Johnny's Thirst had surpassed the need to protect his skin. That was the last time Cole had seen a sunset.

Well, he hadn't actually seen the sun itself—or if he had he didn't remember it. What he remembered were the colors, the violet wisps and gold and pink swirls. But what he recalled most vividly was the way he'd felt, as if he were part of the swirls and they were part of him, and as if he were floating in a glorious dream—perhaps to do with sunsets?—that got more and more satisfyingly intense as he died. Of course, he hadn't realized at the time that he was dying. But when he was half drained—the point at which omnis died—and Johnny had pulled his face away from Cole's neck, gasping, all Cole had felt was sharp regret, and anger at Johnny, not for what he had done, but because he had stopped.

Once the dream was gone he had only a pale memory of it. And then, almost immediately, his Thirst had taken shape, and Johnny'd had to look sharp to keep Cole from killing in his turn.

So had started the endless landscape of the years.

Remembering that floating dream he could well imagine that the omnis enjoyed combining feeding with sex even more than he did.

"You *do* want to combine, don't you?" The words slid out silkily, and Mary Kate tilted her head so that the hair fell away from her neck, baring it as she peered sideways at him.

Before he thought, his eyes were sliding over that bare skin, down to the black lace and back up again.

It *was* tempting. And he *did* need to feed.

He could pull her into the shadows and take advantage of everything she was offering, all at once. It was what she wanted, and there was so much temptation here. The open feeds, the omni's reactions. Seeing the girl slide to the couch, limp and vulnerable. The exposed curve of Mary Kate's neck.

Here in the Building anything he wanted was his, and he wouldn't even have to ask for it. He could let his usual caution slip even more than it already had—there was no hurry; he and Sandor didn't *have* to take Gordon out tonight.

He could wait, and make Mary Kate wait, till Thirst began to uncurl inside his body. He could wait till even the sight of any one of the omnis sent him quivering and he could smell the faint salt and metal through the thin skin over a pulse. *Then* he could let himself have her.

He could. But he knew he wouldn't. He needed to get out of the city as soon as possible. The tantalizing atmosphere of the Building had already begun to seep into him. Just being here took the edge off his thinking.

"I'm sorry, Mary Kate. I would like to feed. But that's all."

She peered up at him for a moment and apparently saw something in his face that told her he meant it, because she dropped the subject.

The dryer was set for thirty minutes, so he *did* allow himself to take his time. There was a metal folding chair leaning against a trunk; he pulled it into the ring of light in front of the machines and sat on it. Then he took Mary Kate's hand and pulled her onto his lap. And this time he used his teeth, but carefully; she offered her wrist, but he held it in his fingers and instead concentrated on the tender skin in the inner crook of her arm. He kissed and sucked on it for a few moments, enjoying the sound of her breath and the scent of her skin and clothes. When he nipped the skin she instantly grew still, and he listened to her breathing and counted the pulses of her heart while he fed slowly, intermittently, thinking of that long-ago dream, always careful of the time and her pulse: not too much, not too little, and with absolute self-control.

When he was done, the dryer wasn't quite finished. Mary Kate's head rested on his shoulder, her arms draped around him. It made him feel as if he was smothering under a blanket, but since she liked it, he let her stay. It was little enough to do.

The basement, with its silence and shadows, its cool dank smell of dust, its memories of centuries, pressed in around him. He thought again about his sketchbooks; he used to draw, but that was before photography, and he had long since tossed away his charcoals and pencils for cameras and film. If he didn't remember the pictures he'd drawn, if he didn't think about the people in them, then no one would. He could almost see them crumbling along with the pages, clutching at the yellowed paper.

But he sat quietly, finishing the moment with Mary Kate.

When the dryer whirled to a stop, he had to ask her to get up. She leaned against the washing machine, watching his movements as he pulled out his clothes. She ran her eyes eagerly over each item of clothing as he folded and laid it carefully in the basket, ready to go upstairs for repacking.

He realized suddenly that she would follow him to four-and-a-half if he took his clothes up now. She would install herself, would stay there while he took Gordon to feed. She would stay there until the moment he packed his belongings and got out of New York.

So he left the basket on top of the dryer and headed up the stairs.

Mary Kate trooped after him.

"I enjoyed it, Mary Kate," he told her as they stood in the hallway, and then added, "Good night." He had to find Sandor so that the two of them could take Gordon on his first hunt.

But Mary Kate picked up Cole's hand, lacing her fingers into his as she leaned against him.

"I need to go now," he told her.

"Do you *have* to?"

"Yes. I have business to attend to."

"What kind of business?"

"Private business. For Johnny."

She nuzzled his chest. "Can't you put it off another night?"

"I'm sorry, but I can't."

"Come and get me when you're done then. Promise?"

"I will if there's time," Cole said; it wasn't *quite* a lie. He opened the door to Johnny's apartment with his free hand and held it for her.

Finally, reluctantly, she let go. She gave him a long look, then walked in.

He made sure she was out of sight before he set

about looking for Sandor. Sometimes it was hard to be firm with omnis. Their lives were already both fragile and short, and treating them rudely had always seemed to Cole to be unnecessarily cruel.

But he'd have to buck up, starting now. Gordon wasn't an omni, but he was close enough that Cole would have to watch his step. Cole could not afford to let his feelings make him tentative about his responsibility. Not this time.

This evening would be a test—not for Gordon, but for Cole himself.

CHAPTER EIGHT

"SHALL we take the subway?" Sandor asked. The three of them stood on the sidewalk in front of the Building. Gordon was silent, with an odd look on his face—something, Cole judged, between fear, embarrassment about last night, and stubborn dignity. He was dressed much the same as he had been before: jeans, T-shirt. He'd nodded to Cole but had not said a word to him.

"Do you know how to get there on the subway?" Cole asked Sandor.

"More or less."

More or less? Cole had a sudden flash of all those colored lines on the subway map. "Let's walk," he said.

"It's at least twenty blocks."

"Let's start walking, and if we see a cab, we'll take

that." It would be just as well, he thought; he could use the time to dive in and start instructing Gordon. He would not be able to speak freely in a taxi, and there was a lot Gordon needed to know.

So he began right away, as they started down the street. "It's always good to feed early in the evening," Cole told Gordon. "That way, if there's some sort of trouble, you still have plenty of time."

Gordon walked along, slouching, hands crammed in his pockets. He did not ask what kind of trouble.

Cole explained anyway. "For example, if you had trouble with an omni, bungled your approach—anything that might cause suspicion or distrust. You must never do anything that makes people look at you askance."

Sandor kept turning to see if any cabs were coming. Gordon was acting as if this was his first time on the streets of Manhattan. The Missouri boy in him was obviously taking everything in: buildings squeezed against the sidewalks, stoops jutting in invitation, asphalt like a river at the bottom of a small canyon of brick and stone. His eyes went avidly to every pedestrian they passed, while the objects of his attention, natives all, kept their focus unwaveringly ahead. But he did not ask any questions.

"This will be the interactive type of feeding," Cole told him. "It involves striking up an acquaintance, flirting, conversation. It's necessary to know how to physically overpower someone too, but you're not ready for that yet. That's a hazardous, last-resort kind of thing. You must be strong for it too. You don't look like you've been working out."

"Yes, here is good news, Gordon," Sandor put in. "You can add muscle quickly now. If you've ever wanted six-pack abs, now you may have them. This is one of the things that's a nice change from being omni," he said encouragingly, as if offering a child a candy bar. "You don't have to work hard at looking ripped."

Gordon was starting to look a little annoyed at all the information, but there was no telling which bits might be crucial at any given moment. So Cole elaborated anyway. "Your muscles tear a little every time you lift weights," he informed Gordon. "Omnis have to wait for the tears to heal, and when they heal, they build muscle. You do not have to wait. What would take an omni months to achieve, you can do in a few days. Hours, if you—"

"Oh, look," Sandor said, stopping at the corner of Ninety-sixth Street. "There's a subway stop. Shall we go down?"

Cole and Gordon stopped, too. Gordon turned his head, searching eagerly till his eyes lighted on the railing that marked the stairway. Apparently he had not seen a subway entrance before.

Cole didn't bother to look. "Only if you know exactly what trains are down there, Sandor. Only if you know precisely which one we get on and exactly where it will end up."

Sandor shook his head. "Where is your sense of adventure?"

"The goal for tonight is to *avoid* adventure," Cole said, and started walking again.

The other two followed.

"Do you have any sort of tool?" Cole asked Gordon.

"I gave him one of my rings," Sandor put in.

"Good." Cole turned to Gordon again. "Have you used it yet?"

"Yes," said Sandor.

"I'm asking Gordon."

"Yeah," said Gordon in a don't-nag-me tone.

"Only in the Building though," Sandor added.

"The world is not the Building," Cole told Gordon. "You must be very careful not to let anyone see the ring with the cap off. Read the situation. If the omni is drunk, you have more leeway than if it's sober. With a sober omni, in a nonsexual situation, you often have exactly one try to get close. You can't go touching their neck over and over, and you certainly can't go putting your face up against them."

"Oh," said Sandor, stopping again. "I'd forgotten about this place." He pointed to a building across the street. "It's much closer than Seth's bar. What do you think?"

Cole looked it over. FROMM'S, the sign said. No windows, so he couldn't see inside. But there was an awning. And the sign was classy, subtly lit cursive on a white board. Not a dive. Cole hoped it wasn't too upscale; he didn't want to drag an uncouth, grumpy, beer-guzzling teenager into a place where he'd stand out—not when he himself looked like a teenager as well. "We can give it a try." He thought quickly as they crossed the street—what else did Gordon need to know before they went in? "Stay away from the wrist," he said. "That's almost useless everywhere except in the Building, because they can see everything you're doing. Sandor, can you think of anything else?"

"No, you're doing wonderfully well. But it reminds me; did you know Mitch has a tongue stud?"

"No."

"He said it doesn't work very well, because it's hard for him to get the cap on and off. And once it's off he has to be careful not to cut up the roof of his mouth."

"And it draws attention as well," Cole pointed out, for Gordon's benefit.

"Not so much these days. But I expect he'll give up on it."

"Probably." They were outside the door now. It opened to let a couple exit, and the heavy thrum of dance music swirled out with them. The couple strolled off holding hands, and the door shut, locking the sound inside again.

Cole turned to Gordon, who he could tell was beginning to feel a little nervous. "Now listen. All you have to do is put your hand on your omni's neck. Don't grab, of course—you mustn't frighten it—but naturally. If you can find its pulse with your fingers, just below the jawline, things will go easier. After you have some experience, you won't have to feel; you'll be able to judge by looking. In any case, you must push the tool in quickly, do you understand? Like this"—Cole demonstrated, in the air—"like punching a hole. Quick and neat. Then you've got to latch on right away, as soon as you make the hole. If you don't, the omni will likely be screaming and perhaps bleeding all over the place. Act quickly; get your mouth on the cut, because that will numb it. Don't go too long; count to— hmm, let's say twenty—as you're feeding. Twenty seconds should be about right for the jugular, and the omni will be none the wiser. Oh." Cole pulled out his wallet. "Here's your ID." He held out the plastic card he'd gotten from Alice.

Gordon stared at it. After a moment he reluctantly took the card between two fingers and studied it more closely.

"This is fake."

"No kidding."

"My birthday's not in October."

"It doesn't matter when your birthday is."

"And I'm not"—he squinted at the card—"twenty-one. I'm eighteen."

"You're as old as you need to be."

"Hey. Does this mean I can buy beer?"

"You may buy beer to your heart's content," Cole said. He did not add that the kid wouldn't want to once he'd tasted it.

"Good," Gordon said, with the first real sign of spirit Cole had seen in him so far. "I'm going to get totally wasted. I'm not going to stop till I pass out. And then when I wake up, I'm going to start all over again."

"You can't."

"Why not? I saw you've got that credit card. It's not even yours, is it? What difference does it make to you if I check out for a bit? God, I deserve it. I—"

"It's not the money. You can't get drunk."

"Oh yeah? Watch me."

"No, I mean it's physically impossible. Alcohol has no effect on you. It might make you sick, if you drink very much—but you won't want to. Now hush and come on."

Cole led the way into Fromm's. It looked larger on the inside, with small round tables surrounding a dance floor and a long bar down one side of the room. Neon signs flashed the names of various beers.

"We'll order drinks," he told Gordon. "Go ahead and

get whatever you like. You can even try to drink it. But the reason it's there is in case something goes wrong, and you need to excuse your behavior to an omni. Best to order from the bar tonight," he said to Sandor.

"Ah, yes, good thinking," said Sandor. "No interruptions by waitresses. See, Gordon, Cole thinks of everything. Now you two sit down, and I'll go."

"I want beer," Gordon said stubbornly. "Something imported."

"Same for me," Cole told Sandor. He had already picked out a table. It was nestled in a corner but had a fairly good view of the room.

He led the way, and Gordon followed, willingly now. Cole watched him as he sat down. The kid looked around the room, and Cole noticed that he tilted his head back slightly—for a heme, the air was threaded with shifting currents of scents: skin, sweat, perfume, salt. And the room wasn't even full, not like it would have been on a weekend. Even this kid's underdeveloped instincts were shifting toward alertness, with the promise of a feed at hand.

That was encouraging, Cole thought. Even if the boy wasn't aware of it.

Cole let his gaze roam around the room, looking for prospects. Sandor came back with the drinks, but Cole ignored him. He'd already zeroed in on a table where four young women sat in varying postures. Two were dressed in jeans. The third wore a short plaid skirt, the fourth an even shorter dress of thin clingy material. They were intent on their conversation, apparently having a good time, not needing anyone else.

Cole heard Gordon sputtering—he'd tried his beer, obviously—but ignored it; Cole was on the hunt, waiting to make eye contact.

The girls burst into laughter, doubling over, and one laid her head on the table.

But another happened to look up, across the room, where she met Cole's gaze.

She grew silent.

Cole smiled.

She stared at him, eyes caught, intent.

Then she slowly smiled back.

Cole turned away. "That's a good place to start," he told Gordon. "Look at all the empty glasses on the table. And see how they're acting? They're half drunk, at least."

Gordon turned to look. Then he shook his head. "Those girls—those girls are out of my league."

"No they're not. Go and introduce yourself. Look into their eyes. Listen to this song—it's slow—so ask one of the girls to dance. This is good luck—tipsy girl, slow dance. You may be able to get done quickly. Be flexible, be alert. Keep your wits about you. And remember," Cole added. "The most important thing is that you won't want to stop when you hit twenty—but you *must*. Let me hear you say it back to me."

"Count to twenty," Gordon repeated, eyes on the girls. "Then stop."

"Good. Good. Now, put on the ring. Ah—nice ring, Sandor."

"That's one of my Ivy League collection."

"So, Gordon, you're now a graduate of Yale. Congratulations. Do you know how to get the top off?"

"Yeah."

"Go ahead and do it now; that's best for your first time. Now turn it so the point is hidden in your palm. That's right."

Gordon gave the girls a frightened, eager look. His breath was coming in quick puffs. When he spoke, it was to himself, not to Cole. "Okay," he said, running his eyes up and down the girl in the clingy dress. "Okay. Count to twenty. Okay."

And he got up and walked stiff legged across the room.

Cole and Sandor watched as he said something to the girl. He looked quite nervous, but the girl was caught in his gaze. She smiled and got up, sliding her hand into his although he hadn't offered it.

"So far so good," Cole heard Sandor say. He didn't answer. He glanced back at the bouncer who stood by the front door, arms crossed, lazily watching the doorman check IDs.

On the dance floor, the girl locked her hands behind Gordon's neck and gazed up into his eyes as she spoke to him. Gordon answered—and then looked over her shoulder to give Cole and Sandor a half-embarrassed, half-furious glare: *Quit spying on me!*

Sandor immediately turned in his seat. "I think our boy is finding his land legs, so to speak," he said, sounding relieved.

Cole didn't bother to look away. Someone needed to keep an eye on things.

Because Gordon wasn't making his move. He didn't even seem to be able to talk to the girl. Every time she said anything, his lips moved in a monosyllable, and then he went back to dancing silently—not dancing, really, Cole thought, more like shuffling from foot to foot. He was too obviously working his hands up her back and couldn't quite seem to figure out how to get the ring to its target. His face began to look more and more desperate until the song was ending, when he finally put one hand on the back of his partner's neck.

She gave a muffled cry and jerked back, clapping one hand to the spot he'd pricked. "What the hell are you doing?" she said, so sharply that Cole and Sandor could hear her from where they sat. It didn't help that the music had stopped. "What's wrong with you?" Her eyes were narrow with suspicion. She didn't walk away, though; she was caught between indignation and whatever it was in a heme's eyes that drew omnis in the first place, whatever it was that kept her from smacking him and stomping off.

The ring had also done its work, Cole could see, because Gordon was becoming quite undone. The girl was now looking at the fingers she'd pressed to the

101

wound, and it was obvious they had a bit of blood on them, because Gordon looked for all the world as if he wanted to bite off her fingertips.

Cole knew the kid couldn't possibly be feeling any Thirst; he'd fed just last night. No, what had happened was that two weeks of indulgence had conditioned him to instant gratification. His ring had released the coppery, tantalizing scent of her blood, and already he was salivating like Pavlov's dog.

Sandor pushed back his chair, ready to get up and help, but Cole put a hand on his arm. "No harm done yet," he said in a low voice. "Let him try to work his way out of his own mess. See if he has the sense to get himself under control."

And, miracle of miracles, Gordon did.

First he tore his gaze away from the tempting fingers. And he resisted the temptation to look at her neck, Cole noted. No, the boy wasn't hopeless. Not completely, anyway.

Then he said something, spreading his hands out in a gesture of apology. He kept eye contact—that was good. It might even be enough to keep her with him.

No. "Just get away from me," the girl said in a loud voice, and walked off the dance floor.

Sandor watched Gordon with pity. "We should help him."

"No," said Cole. "Not yet."

A shamefaced Gordon slid into his chair with Cole and Sandor.

"You've got to be quicker," Cole said immediately. "If you'd gotten your mouth on fast enough, that girl wouldn't have noticed anything at all."

"She was so hot," Gordon said, depressed again. "I've never had a girl that hot act interested in me."

Sandor grinned. "Get used to it."

Gordon's head shot up. "What do you mean?"

"Oh ho, my friend, you haven't noticed? We are an attractive people."

"I don't look any different."

"It's the attitude. Something in the eyes, the smile. You must smile more now. Isn't that so, Cole?"

"Yes, but not all the time or you'll look like a moron."

"My attitude hasn't changed," Gordon said. "Except I'm a fucking miserable loser with no home now."

"You don't see it," Sandor said, "but already you move with more confidence. You make eye contact and hold it, but without seeming odd about it. People are attracted to our kind. The more so as we get older."

Gordon stared gloomily at his full beer glass. Then Sandor's words seem to really sink in, and he looked across the table at Sandor with the first sign of interest Cole had seen in him thus far. "You're serious? You mean I can get hot girls now?"

"No," Cole said quickly. "You're not getting hot anything. Right now you are to concentrate on *feeding*. Beginners are not concerned with hotness. You'd better start off with homely omnis. Look for the less attractive ones in a group, the ones left behind when their good-looking friends are up dancing. Those are the ones that are easiest to get close to, and quickly. And the drunker the better."

"Can I get a buzz off a drunk one?"

"No. You are done with all that. You are here to feed and nothing more."

"God. I can't get drunk. I can't go after hot girls. According to you, I can't die. I can't go home, because— because everything's messed up. I can't do anything."

"You can have sex," Sandor said. "Plenty of sex—isn't that nice? And you can't get sick," he added helpfully. "And you can't get a girl pregnant, so no need for those things, those what-do-you-call-thems."

"What he means to say is that you are sterile," Cole pointed out.

So many emotions were flickering across Gordon's face, it was hard to separate them. Was he surprised? Upset? Angry? Disbelieving? He reminded Cole of a cartoon character whose head is about to explode.

"Anyway, try again," Cole said. "Look at that girl over there, the one at the bar. See, in the black dress? Take your time. You still feel all right, don't you? Why don't you go sit and talk to her for a few minutes."

But Gordon failed again. This time the girl screeched and then started yelling. All eyes were on Gordon now, and the big guy by the door headed toward him.

Cole and Sandor jumped up to intervene. Apologizing profusely for their drunken friend, they walked him out, one on each side.

Outside the door, they stopped. The sidewalk under the awning was brightly lit. All three were silent.

"Well," said Cole. "Let's move on, shall we?" He looked up the street, thinking.

"It would be better if this was a weekend," Sandor mused. "Tuesdays are not a night for people letting their hair down."

Cole ignored him. "Look over there, at that place." There was another awning over windows tinted dark, with neon lights against the gloom. "Let's check it out. Gordon, how are you feeling?"

"Fine. Just—you know." He shifted on his feet. "Fine."

"Come on." Cole started walking. "It's been a bit tantalizing, is all. Are you still in control?"

"Yes. I'm ready, though," Gordon admitted.

"Good. Keep your focus."

"Yeah."

The three of them entered the bar. This one was heavy with polished wood, with mirrors and glass and bright loops and swirls of colored neon on the walls. Cole ordered drinks—or decoys, as Sandor called them—and found a corner table.

Gordon didn't even pick up his drink. He hunched over the table, muttering to himself. "I can do this. I can do this." Finally he stood up. "I can do this," he told Cole and Sandor, and walked off.

But he couldn't. For the next hour or so, Cole and Sandor watched him fumble his way around the room, awkwardly trying to start conversations. Finally he was back, drooping again.

"I just can't get close enough to anybody. Not without getting really perverted." He was beginning to sound desperate. "Let's just go back. I don't see why we even need to do this."

Cole and Sandor traded glances. "He's only going to get sloppier," Cole remarked.

"I'll get one started," Sandor said. "Give me a moment." He pushed his chair back with a screech and headed toward the bathrooms.

Cole waited a minute or so, then got up. "Come on," he told Gordon.

In the small hallway by the restrooms, Sandor stood behind a man who had been using the phone between the two bathrooms. Sandor couldn't really look up, because he had his mouth on the man's neck, but evidently he could see them coming, because one hand gestured wildly at Gordon, motioning him forward.

Gordon didn't move. Cole gave him a little shove, and he finally headed over. There was a bit of jostling as Sandor and Gordon switched positions, but otherwise the transfer was made without incident.

"Big guy," Sandor commented, standing beside Cole

with arms folded. "I think Gordon could go a little longer, don't you?"

"Gordon," Cole said, enunciating carefully, "you can count to thirty instead of twenty."

He counted silently to himself, noticing that Sandor's lips were moving also. He could hear the person on the other end of the line saying, "Hello? Hello?" The man stood there in a state of dazed bliss.

"When you're done," Cole told Gordon, "step away and walk off quickly. You've got a couple of seconds before he's aware again."

"I'll meet you back at the table," Sandor said over his shoulder as he walked away.

"Thanks," Cole told him, backing away from Gordon and his feed. He was ready to step in if the guy had to be quieted. He hoped Gordon could at least get off without making a scene.

And—another miracle—Gordon did. He simply let go and stepped away, and then he was smoothly walking out of the hallway and back into the bar.

Cole followed casually behind. He saw the man's expression—fear and wonder. There was never any telling what the omnis thought about this sort of thing.

Cole figured most of them dismissed it pretty quickly, but then he also wondered if it stayed with them, if sometimes they took it for some sort of religious experience. Or perhaps some form of stroke or seizure.

As he sat down at the table, he decided to give the kid a "Nicely done" for the few things he had done right tonight. Just so the boy would know that he *did* have some skills that could be built on.

But Gordon spoke first.

"You know," he said, twirling a cardboard coaster around and around, "I really don't like you guys watching me like that. It's totally perverted."

"Sorry," said Sandor. "We wanted to make sure you didn't go too long."

"And that guy tasted funny," Gordon complained.

This annoyed Cole, but Sandor nodded, unperturbed. "He'd had Italian for dinner," he explained helpfully. Then, in answer to the look Gordon gave him, he added, "You can always tell, because of the garlic. Curry is even stronger."

Cole decided he would *not* compliment Gordon after all. "You can't even get your own feeds," he told him, "so you have no right to gripe about the service. And I don't believe you thanked Sandor for helping you out of a jam."

"Oh no, Cole, that's all right," Sandor said.

"It's not all right. It's rude, that's what it is."

"Thanks," Gordon mumbled at Sandor.

"You're welcome," Sandor said quickly.

"But this is so stupid," Gordon added. "What's the point? It's, like, really hard. And humiliating. And it's gross. That guy was gross. He had a pimple on his neck. Back at the Building all I have to do is sit there and girls come asking me—"

"Omnis are not your own personal smorgasbord," Cole said.

But he'd decided. Johnny had been right: Cole's earlier failure *had* stemmed from an entirely different situation. That difference was quite clear now that he'd worked with the kid a little. With Bess he'd been mucking around in his own emotions, wanting to make her happy rather than pushing her toward independence.

With Gordon there were no complications or distractions. The kid was childish and pouty, but Cole could deal with that. Taking him on his first road trip would not be easy, but Cole could do that too.

"We need to get going," he told Sandor. "We'll go back

just long enough to pack, and then we're going to get out of town. We'll replay this over and over again, every night, until he gets it right."

"You mean leave tonight?"

"Yes. He needs to be out of the Building. *Now*," Cole added with certainty. "The longer he's there, the more he has to unlearn. Sandor, he has to fight for control *just from the scent of a puncture*."

"Oh. That's not good."

"No. It looks to me as if he's been feeding multiple times a night. He's like an unweaned baby. Gordon," he said, "you are to feed once a night. No more, no less."

Gordon looked from one face to the other, bewildered, very omni-like. Cole said nothing, but pushed his chair back and rose to leave. He was ready—ready to be severe, even brutal if necessary. As quickly as possible, the kid had to absorb the fact that he had an eternity of self-discipline ahead of him.

CHAPTER NINE

COLE had everything laid out in neat piles on his bed: jeans and knit shirts rolled up like sausages, ready to go into the backpack; dress shirt, slacks, and tie—which he hadn't used—folded and set aside; shampoo and shaving gear sealed into a large plastic bag.

That was when he heard the knock.

The door to four-and-a-half had many locks, but he'd only fastened one, just enough to keep any omnis from strolling in. Now he opened the door a crack to see who it was.

Johnny.

Cole opened the door all the way. There was no one else on the landing. "Everything all right?"

"Everything's fine. I just wanted to have a private word with you before you left."

Cole nodded. He stepped back, and Johnny followed him in. "Do you want to sit down?" Cole asked.

"No. Go on with whatever you're doing. Don't let me interrupt."

So Cole led the way to the bedroom. The room was back exactly as he'd found it upon arrival, except for his clothes scattered on the bed. That, and he'd taken the cover off the window.

All the windows in the Building had them: wooden covers that fit perfectly into the window frames, overlapping the walls a few inches on all sides. All were meticulously constructed so that they could not fall, but Johnny would take no risks—he'd also had each window fitted with bolts that clamped the covers on.

Cole had not only removed the cover of the bedroom window, he had opened the window itself earlier, when he'd gotten up. It was hard to sleep well with the occupied apartment on the fifth floor just a few steps away; sometimes the ceiling felt like a live thing hovering over him, pressing down. It was always a relief when the clock said night had arrived and he could at least open the window. The only thing visible outside was the brick wall of the building opposite, but he felt he could breathe more deeply with fresh air coming in, and some of the tension that had collected while tossing and turning would drain from his shoulders and neck.

Now Johnny came over to lean against one of the bedposts. "I appreciate your help on this, Cole," he said, watching Cole place the rolled-up clothes side by side on top of his shoes.

Cole knew he meant Gordon. He nodded but said nothing. It would do no good to unload on Johnny.

"Something to remember," Johnny said. "New hemes are always afraid."

Cole shot him a glance. "Afraid of what?"

"Of being left alone. Being left behind. When they change over, they lose everything in just seconds—everything they thought was real and true about themselves and their world. Even more so with Gordon. Sandor was not able to get to him in time, you see, and there was some violence. Gordon's had his whole life ripped away from him. You and Sandor are the only way he has of making sense of it all. He may not like that, but he's going to know it's true, deep down. And if he gets . . ."—Johnny hesitated—". . . difficult, you can use that fear to your advantage."

Cole thought about it as he picked up his leather file

case. He vaguely recalled feeling a nameless, wordless panic when Johnny had left him alone for brief periods of time in those early days.

Johnny eyed the case as Cole dropped it into an outside pocket of his backpack. "Still taking your photographs, I see."

"Not so much anymore." In fact, he had not taken any in years.

"I always thought they were a good idea. It's too easy to get dulled to the world. It's our ability to feel that keeps us human."

Cole didn't know what to say to that. He gave Johnny a brief, tight-lipped smile, then put his dress clothes inside the backpack, tucking them around the casual clothes that were already packed.

"I wanted to tell you, too, that if Gordon gets completely out of hand, Cole—if you feel he's becoming a danger to the rest of us—"

And there it was, laid out in all its ugly nakedness: What could happen if Cole failed.

For the good of society, a mad dog had to be put down. No matter if one liked animals, no matter if the dog in question was a beloved pet. It must be humanely put to sleep in order to protect the rest.

Of course, a heme couldn't be put down exactly. Johnny had done it once that Cole knew of. Cole hadn't been there, but he knew the story. One of the Old World hemes had appeared, bringing with him a firmly entrenched belief in his right to feed to the death whenever he wanted. He'd left a trail of new hemes behind him; that's where Alice, Seth, and Elise had come from. No amount of talking made a dent in his conviction that he had no obligation to anyone but himself.

Johnny had locked him in a shed—a shed without windows but with cracks between the boards. Not full sun—that was why the screaming had lasted for a few days. The poor sod had healed a little each night until finally the sun took him. Johnny said that guy had torn at the boards of the shed with his bare hands; Johnny had found broken-off fingernails among the splinters on the ground.

It wasn't something the Colony hemes liked to remember. Cole certainly didn't want to think about it, and he hoped to God he wouldn't have to anytime soon.

"I know what needs to be done," he told Johnny. "And I'll find a way to do it."

"I didn't mean that. I meant that you can call me. And I'll come. I don't ask anyone to do something I won't do myself."

"I can handle it," Cole said, stubborn. No matter how horrible this got, he would not dump it on Johnny. He had already shirked his responsibilities; he had done nothing to help in the apartment on the fifth floor. Ever.

He owed Johnny so much—owed them all, but especially Johnny.

"I know you can handle it. But I don't think it'll come to that. I honestly believe that the boy will do fine, with you and Sandor there. And," Johnny said with a grin, "I'm always right, don't you know?"

Cole didn't smile back. He could almost feel the burden settling into place onto his shoulders.

"Sandor has a cell phone," Johnny said lightly, changing the subject. "I wish you'd start carrying one too."

"No thanks."

The bed was empty now, except for the backpack and his wallet lying next to it. Cole picked up the wallet and opened it. "I expect we'll be back in a few months." All of his Colony-owned credit cards were there, plus a bit of cash. Bookstore discount cards. His driver's license—state of California.

"Any particular destinations?" Johnny asked as Cole slid the wallet into his back pocket.

"No. We'll avoid Missouri, of course—that's where Gordon is from, right?"

"Yes. And it wouldn't surprise me if the police were looking for him."

Cole gave Johnny a sharp look. But he did not ask; he wanted to get Gordon out of here, get himself out of here, get this thing started.

He'd be stuck in cars and hotels with Sandor and Gordon for hours on end. There would be plenty of time to hear what had happened to the kid.

"I figure once we're out on the highway, we'll wander a bit." He checked his backpack, making sure nothing was sticking out that might get caught in the zipper. "We'll move every night, at first. After Gordon gets the hang of things, maybe we can slow down."

"You like the West Coast."

"Yes. I don't know whether we'll head there or not. Well," he added, zipping his backpack shut in one practiced movement, "I guess I'm ready." He lifted the backpack and swung it over his shoulder.

Johnny didn't move but remained leaning with one shoulder against the post. "Do you have any questions, Cole?"

About Gordon? About how to subdue him if he got out of control?

About the fifth floor?

"No," Cole said. "No questions. Are you coming down to see us off?"

"No, I'll finish up in here."

"Shall I shut the window?"

"No." Johnny gave him another grin. "I'll close up the place. You go tend to our Accident. I know you, Cole, and I'm not worried. I know you'll do it."

This time Cole managed a short smile back. "Right. Still . . . wish me luck."

"Good luck."

They didn't shake hands, didn't hug. Cole just left, sliding his other arm into the backpack strap as he headed toward the door. When he looked back, Johnny was lifting the cover into the window frame.

Outside four-and-a-half, Cole ran easily down the stairs. On the fourth floor, as he waited for the elevator, he glanced up the long flight to the fifth. He hadn't even asked how things were. He could still go up there, quickly drop in. Somebody would be sitting with her, reading or watching television in the silence.

But that would be pointless. Painful for him, and nothing at all to her.

He decided he would not stop by the downstairs apartment on the way out either. Sandor was big on good-byes, and hellos too, but Cole and Johnny were alike in not caring much about either. Cole knew he would see everyone again. They might have different haircuts or hair colors, different clothes, different things to talk about (except Frederick). But, aside from superficial details, everyone had always been the same, and always would be.

That's just the way it was. Nothing changed, not even in the apartment on the fifth floor. No more change than a rock. Except that a rock got to melt sometimes and turn into lava—or be eroded to bits, into sand. Rocks got to make islands and mountains.

Even a rock, Cole thought as the doors opened before him and he stepped into the elevator for the interminable ride down, *has it over us*.

PART TWO

The Road

CHAPTER TEN

COLE wanted to do all the driving. He didn't want to be a passenger; he was used to being behind the wheel—used to watching the road, keeping track of the maps, checking signs, making decisions.

So they took Cole's Accord.

Gordon hadn't said a word the whole way to the park-and-ride. Once they were on the road, he politely answered any questions asked of him. But mostly he just sat.

That was good. Wasn't it? Sure. The quieter the kid was, the better. Because the less he talked, the more he could listen.

Now that they were out of the Building they were in no hurry, having no destination, and stopped for the day after only a few hours, at a motel on the highway. Sandor and Gordon shared a room—after all, Gordon couldn't be left alone—but Cole asked for a single at the desk. He was on edge. He'd been around people for two whole nights now. He craved solitude.

He made himself wait to see Sandor and Gordon safely into their room. When their door clicked shut behind them and he heard Sandor slide the bolt into place, he turned and went to his own room.

Finally he was by himself. He flipped on the light by the door, then turned the dead bolt and pushed the hinged lock into position. He had his suitcase now and was ready to switch everything over from his backpack. But—first things first—he set the backpack on the bed by the window and pulled the drapes closed. Then he unzipped a side pocket and pulled out a small travel bag. Inside were the duct tape and scissors. Carefully he set about sealing the edges of the curtains to the walls, shutting out the sky.

Next, he grabbed the inevitable hotel pad of paper by the phone and wrote down the name of the city: Springfield, New Jersey. Sometimes, on the road, the towns would run together into a blur. It was disorienting to wake up and not know where he was. And it was awkward—drew attention—when he had to ask.

Now he moved everything over to the suitcase. When that was done, he dropped onto the hard boxlike mattress, locked his hands behind his head, and stared at the ceiling. He did not want the TV on; he wanted quiet.

He lay there for a while, trying to let the silence soak into his bones. But he couldn't seem to relax.

The hotel felt even blander than hotels usually did, after the eccentricities of the Building and its occupants. This place seemed exactly like what it was, a stopover for people on their way to other places.

He got up to take a shower and came out in shorts and a T-shirt, hair damp. He didn't bother to comb his hair but shuffled through the ever-changing collection of paperback books he always had with him. He read almost every night into the morning; reading was his comfort and his companion. Lately he was on a Mount Everest kick. He had no desire to go there himself, but he liked reading about it.

Tonight, though, his thoughts seemed to skitter around, unable to find a place to rest. He didn't feel like reading.

He set aside the books. He knew he should probably start planning for the worst. He *always* made plans for worse-case scenarios—made a plan, then tucked it away, feeling safer in the knowledge that it lay ready for use if need be: What would he do if an omni saw him feeding and confronted him? What if his car broke down, and he was stuck by the side of the road with dawn coming? The worst case almost never happened, but having a plan was what kept one from having to scramble, panicked, at the last second.

Well. Of course he was going to make damn sure to do right by Gordon. But . . . if worse *did* come to worst . . .

Locking someone in a shed wouldn't work anymore. People lived so close together these days, screams would be heard. You'd have to get a heme away from the towns and the omnis. Maybe a field? Wouldn't you have to immobilize the heme—and how would you do that? Well, you'd have to . . . have to . . .

He thought of his own burned skin, hanging in whitened shreds.

Stop it, he told himself. This sort of thinking distracted from the problem at hand.

But . . . if he did what he was supposed to do, there

wouldn't *be* any problem. All he had to do was remain focused on his task. All he had to do was his job.

He had the knowledge to make it so, and he certainly had the determination.

So he deliberately put the thought away and stretched out on the floor at the foot of the bed. He did some sit-ups, some crunches, and various kinds of push-ups—not too many though. It drew attention if you were overly bulked up. He only needed strength enough to correct a feeding gone wrong.

When that was done he sat on the carpeted floor and stared at his toes for a bit.

Perhaps I should have gone to see her.

He *had* seen her for one moment, right after Johnny brought her back. She'd been in bad shape—sun damage in hemes took longer to heal than other injuries, and Bess had been so badly burned that it actually left scars. The bones hadn't been set before they healed. And her eyes! The pupils were permanently dilated, and the irises that used to be expressive brown had stretched to mere rims around clear black. They had become empty, flat. Inhuman as two marbles. She had no idea whether anyone else was in the room or not.

Seeing her that way had stricken him to the heart—a physical pain, a stone that lodged in his chest. Even now, a hundred and twenty years later, the lump still hadn't melted away.

It wouldn't have made any difference even if I'd visited her, he reminded himself. It was true, an incontrovertible fact. There was no point in going over and over it in his mind. He hadn't been able to connect with her even when he'd wanted to desperately and she'd still been capable of it. Now it was pointless—she was an empty shell, and he didn't want to connect with anybody at all.

He got up and went over to his suitcase. He unzipped the outer pocket and took out his leather file case, then sat down on the floor again to open it.

He ran one hand over the smooth black surface. He had not looked at his photos in a while; but the events of the past two days had made him feel like too many thoughts were battering at his brain, trying to break him into pieces.

It was better to be disconnected. It was easier to maintain control, to live in moderation, when you kept at a distance. The only difficulty with that was a blurring of the years; just like Johnny had said, everlasting life tended to bring with it a loss of feeling. Any being that cannot die must eventually struggle to keep from being dead *inside*.

One had to keep feeling *something*.

Reading was for losing oneself, for forgetting. His photos were for connecting, but safely, without running any risks.

Cole opened the leather case and, digging into a pocket, pulled out one of the many stacks. He would thin out the files a bit. Now was a good time.

Soon black-and-white photos lay scattered around him, like tiles in a mosaic. It had been a while since he'd taken any; if he picked up the habit again, he knew he probably ought to go digital. Then this file case would go into the basement where the sketchbooks were now—the ones that had survived the years anyway. Time had a way of turning pages into dust.

He shuffled through the stack of photos in his hand. There was one of a little boy in a small white coffin. He remembered that one—early 1900s? He'd set himself up as a photographer, and the boy's mother had wanted a picture. People dealt with death head-on back then;

they'd had to. Now it was so sanitized; people died in some nice clean hospital bed, and the body was carted off to be fixed up in private, and a lot of the time no one was there to watch it go into the ground.

Cole looked again at the hollow-cheeked toddler, thin in his white sailor suit, very final, lying in his white box; and he thought he'd keep this one, not for the picture itself, but because of the mother. It was the same urge that had driven him to look back at the lady disappearing down the subway stairs two nights ago. The omnis went away so fast, leaving few traces—and those disappearing so quickly that the only things about them that remained were whatever Cole could hold on to in his own head.

The mother of the boy in this picture was certainly dead herself by now, but as long as he could still look at this photo and remember, then her encounter with adamant and unyielding death still mattered. Without Cole, it would have long ago been lost in the overwhelming current of tragedies and joys that disappeared every day, every hour, every minute.

Used to be, he felt like a weird distorted god, a chronicler of life cycles he could never be part of, a keeper of memories and feelings that everyone else had forgotten.

But more and more, he merely felt as if he were playing solitaire.

He tucked the photo back into the file and looked at the next picture—a farm girl with flyaway hair and tired eyes. He felt nothing when he looked at her and couldn't remember anything about taking the picture, so into the discard pile it went.

CHAPTER ELEVEN

THE next evening Cole opened his eyes to the familiar chink of fluorescent light coming under the door from the hallway. He blinked, and squinted across the white expanse of sheet. Then he raised his head. Sat up. Swung his feet to the floor. Got up. Pulled the duct tape from the curtains. Outside it was dark.

And so it began again.

Sandor opened the door to Cole's knock. The windows were unsealed, the heavy drapes opened to reveal sheer curtains, and through those were the parking lot and streets beyond—halos of lights amid still pools of dark.

Sandor was fully dressed, his suitcase packed and standing near the door. Gordon's suitcase was open on one of the beds, and from the closed bathroom door Cole could hear the shower running.

"Have a seat, Cole." Sandor plopped himself on the bed and leaned back against the headboard, legs stretched out before him. The TV was on a news program.

"Want me to take your bag out to the car?"

Sandor shrugged. "We'll be going out ourselves in a bit. Sit down, relax. There's no hurry."

Cole rolled his suitcase over by Sandor's and sat in the spindly hard-backed chair by the desk.

"Mm. Earthquake in Turkey," Sandor said, eyes on the TV. "Terrible tragedy."

The sound of the shower stopped. "Good." Cole stood up. "He's done."

Sandor didn't move. "Don't count on it."

After a few moments, a blow-dryer started up in the bathroom. Cole sat down again. He wondered how the kid had slept last night, his first real night on the road. Not that Cole was concerned. It was just that if Gordon were tired, it would show in his eyes—it might make him look ill, which was not conducive to luring omnis close.

133

The TV blared an ad for a prime-time drama. "Oh, I mustn't miss that," Sandor said. "Lindsay is going to tell Justin that she doesn't love him anymore."

"How can you stand this stuff?" Cole asked. "Those are supposed to be teenagers, right? But you can tell that not one of them is under twenty-five. Look at that receding hairline!"

"If you watched it, you would get caught up in the story and not notice such things."

"I can't get caught up in it. Real people don't talk like that, in semicolons. And all those people cry so beautifully, without sniffling."

"And how do you cry, Cole?"

"I don't. Listen, there's something I wanted to ask you, Sandor. What was Gordon's first feed? How did that go?"

"It was . . ." Sandor found the remote beside him and clicked off the television. The blow-dryer whined on behind the bathroom door. "It was most unfortunate. I was not quick enough—I was unwell, you see, from being drained, and then the surfeit. He got away from me."

"And what happened?"

"I think he had been going to see his girlfriend, and

that's where he was heading when the Thirst hit. I caught up to him at her apartment door, and he had already started feeding. It wasn't pretty. I had to punch him in the head several times to get him to release her."

"And the girl?"

"It was a bit of a mess, but she was alive. I carried her inside. She was . . . quite messy. He tore at her; you know how it is. Fortunately the bleeding stopped as soon as I knocked him away. Otherwise we would have been in real trouble. As it was we left her there, and I got him away. He was covered in blood, you know. All over his face, his shirt, his hands. And his girlfriend half dead. Poor boy. I don't blame him for being a bit shell-shocked."

Shell-shocked indeed. Poor boy was right.

"Do you think she was okay?" Cole asked.

"Oh yes. Eventually, she would be. Nothing nature couldn't cure. After a while," Sandor added, but he didn't sound too sure. "Do you know, Cole, I think that omni girl in the Building really upset him, the one he took too much from. I think perhaps it reminded him of what happened with his girlfriend."

"Oh?"

"Yes. I thought he was almost adjusting, up till then. Yes, I'm sure it reminded him of that first time." Sandor was still sitting with his legs outstretched, but now he crossed his arms in front of him. "The whole thing got out of hand so quickly. I'm sure it was difficult for his girlfriend when she woke up. I did change her blouse. I debated about that, Cole, because I thought perhaps it was wrong to undress a voluptuous young lady while she was out cold. But I decided it was better that she not wake up to a bloody mess all over her front. Besides, it would have ruined her bedspread. So I took the ruined blouse and put it in a Dumpster on the way back to Gordon's dorm."

"Did Gordon help you with all this?"

"Oh no, he was crouched in a corner. He was not quite all there, if you know what I mean. I can't even imagine what he must have felt. One moment a carefree boy, the next tearing chunks out of a loved one's flesh with your nails and teeth. It makes you feel for him, doesn't it? But I got to him as fast as I could, Cole. I feel terrible about it, but I really did do my best under the circumstances."

"It was a difficult situation," Cole agreed.

"I felt I had to get him out of there quickly," Sandor fretted. "She was out cold, they were both bloody, and he told me that she had a roommate."

"Don't worry about it, Sandor. You did the right thing. He wouldn't have been in any shape to talk to the police."

"Yes, they came looking for him, right off the bat. It was in the newspapers for a few days, until they picked up that incident in Florida—did you see that? The man who killed his boss and served him at the corporate banquet? He fried the fingers up like chicken wings. Anyway, I felt bad for leaving the girl in such a condition, but—ah, well."

"What did you do about his first feed after that?"

In the bathroom, the blow-dryer stopped abruptly.

"A prostitute," Sandor whispered, as he turned to sit on the side of the bed. "I felt it would be easiest."

"Yes, of course."

Sandor frowned in the general direction of his feet. "Cole," he said quickly, "I never asked if he loved her. His girlfriend, I mean. Do you think I should have?"

Marble-blank eyes. Skin crisscrossed with old scars.

"No," Cole said firmly. "It doesn't matter anymore."

"It'll be harder for him to adjust if he's grieving over a lost love."

"He's not going to be doing any grieving on my watch. He's got to stay focused on the present."

"If he's sad, he's sad. Grief is the price one pays for love."

"Not for Gordon," Cole said. "Not anymore."

At that moment Gordon emerged from the bathroom. He was completely dried and dressed, holding a bundle of dirty clothes and hair care products. He had on non-descript khaki pants and a white T-shirt.

He gave Cole a brief nod as he walked over and dumped everything into his suitcase. He wasn't tidy, but he seemed to know what to do. He zipped his bag, sealing the disarray inside, and was ready to go in less than a minute.

"All right." Cole stood and pushed the chair back under the desk. "Let's try again," he told Gordon. Some other time he'd explain it to Sandor: Grief and love were the same thing because they both led to mistakes. Therefore they were luxuries no heme could afford.

.   .

Gordon finally managed to get an independent feed at a billiard hall–arcade somewhere between Springfield and Berkeley Heights.

Cole and Sandor had already taken care of themselves, although Cole did not care for his omni, having accidentally gotten hold of a smoker. He did not like the way nicotine affected the flavor of a feed, and he hated the way smokers smelled, the way their odors seeped into his clothes and hair. He did not let it stop him from getting his evening feed though. The whole place smelled like smoke anyway.

Gordon was learning to use his smile and his eyes. After a couple of abortive attempts, he managed to get into a game of pool with a girl he'd never seen before. He got her when she paused, leaning on her cue stick, waiting for him to pass behind her to get to *his* shot. He leaned over, his hand swiftly at her neck. She gave a brief yelp of surprise, but it was cut off almost instantly by Gordon's mouth.

He stood behind her, one hand on her waist, the other sliding up to rest on her shoulder. Cole, sitting at a table not far away, resisted the urge to remind him to count to twenty. Instead, he started counting to himself, keeping track silently.

But along about thirteen, he noticed something strange. Gordon's fingers were moving on the girl's shoulder. He looked as if he was giving her a one-handed massage. It was an odd way to feed—poor technique, wasted movements, drew attention—and Cole was a little perturbed until he saw the reason for it.

Gordon was looking down her shirt. *He must have a good view,* Cole thought—she was well endowed, and the top three buttons were unfastened. Gordon didn't even seem to be aware that his fingers were moving. Next, Cole thought, he would start drooling. Or playing with himself.

Gordon *was* keeping track of the time though; he released the girl at the proper moment and stepped away.

Then he continued playing pool with her as if nothing had happened.

Sandor nudged Cole. "*That* was well done."

Cole just shook his head.

When the game was done, Gordon came bounding over. He had lost at pool, but he didn't seem to care. He sat down and pounded the tabletop with his fist. "Now *that's* what I'm talking about," he said, beaming at Cole. "Not some smelly guy. Not some wrinkled old hag. Wow. You know, those girls back at the Building, they let you do anything at all. But you could do it out here too, couldn't you? And they'd never know! I could have put my hands—"

"No, you couldn't," Cole cut in. "I saw you *thinking* it, but you are not to *do* it. You're a parasite, not a predator. And definitely not a pervert."

"But nobody's going to know—"

"Your job is to remain as invisible and unobtrusive as possible. That does not include fondling your feeds in a public place."

"Okay, but in private—"

"You are not going to molest people. You're going to treat your feeds with the same respect you'd give them if they were aware."

"But what difference does it make? If they don't know—"

"Because you are a human being and not an animal. Because our lives are built on their backs, and we owe them civility at least."

Gordon's jaw set. He picked up his beer, took a sip—

and choked, then spit the mouthful back into the glass. "I'm not really a human *or* an animal, am I?" He wiped his mouth with the back of his hand. "I'm a vampire."

Silence, frigid and sudden, dropped over the table.

Sandor's mouth tightened, and he would not meet Gordon's eyes. Cole didn't care to look at him either, right now, but he could feel Gordon's confusion, his gaze darting from Sandor to Cole and back again. The kid knew he'd said something wrong.

Cole said nothing. He kept his own face smooth and expressionless.

Sandor and Cole got up at the same time. Gordon followed suit, every line of his body filled with uneasiness.

No one said a word as they walked to the car.

"We do not use that word," Sandor said when they were all inside.

"Which word?" Gordon asked, huddled in the backseat.

"The one you said. The one that starts with a *V*."

"But why not?"

"Because it is not who we are. It bears a thousand connotations that have nothing to do with us."

"It's degrading," Cole said, his voice curt. "It's demeaning. It's a caricature. Got it?"

"I—I guess so."

"We are hemovores," Sandor explained. "*Hemo*, meaning blood. *Vorare*, meaning to devour. You have heard the words *carnivore*, *herbivore*, *omnivore*? We are *hemes*, all the other people are *omnis*."

"This is not a cartoon," Cole said. "It's life. Your life is not a video game, or a movie, or a book."

"Life seldom is," Sandor remarked. "Even for omnis."

"Sorry," said Gordon faintly. "I didn't know."

Cole gave Sandor a look. For over two weeks the kid had apparently gone around thinking he was Dracula.

"It hadn't come up," Sandor explained, apologetic.

Cole fastened his seat belt, and started the car. "There is nothing magical about us," he told Gordon, watching in the mirror to make sure the boy buckled up. "Nothing supernatural."

"We have a disease," Sandor explained.

"But I'm not sick," Gordon said.

"Sick is in the eye of the beholder. It's a very smart germ that creates us. Surely a viral infection, like AIDS or malaria, but transmitted by saliva in the bloodstream.

But this virus is a clever one. It changes your metabolism; it makes you heal, and you don't age. Foolish viruses destroy their hosts. This one makes you live."

"If it's a virus," Gordon argued, "then why doesn't everyone catch it?"

"Obviously," Cole told him, "it can only be transmitted at—or right before—the moment of death."

"Around the time your heart stops beating," Sandor corrected. "Notice you were not dead enough to have brain damage." He sat up as if struck by an idea. "Gordon. You should continue your college education, study the matter. Not enough is known. There are a couple of Norwegian hemes who have been doing research, but they are very thorough and move slowly. You could join them, and be the one to learn all!"

"Me? I'm new to this. Why not you?"

"Oh, I'm not smart enough. And I like my life the way it is. I don't consider myself to be a problem that needs a solution, and I certainly don't need the answer to every question on this earth. Life would be dull if one had all the answers, do you not agree?" He turned back to Cole. "Guess what Gordon was studying in college?"

"I have no idea."

"Premed!" Sandor said. "Now isn't that interesting?"

"How were your grades?" Cole asked.

"Um. Not so good. The teachers, they give tests, but they only tell you about it once, like at the beginning of the semester. So if you forget you're screwed." The lights from passing cars slid over Gordon's shoulders and face, dropping into shadows.

"Did it ever occur to you to write it down?"

"Well, you know. Sometimes I kind of overslept, and I'd have to run, and then I'd forget my notebook and stuff."

Cole could not for the life of him think of anything to say to that. He wondered if Sandor's throat-slitting pickpocket was this clueless.

Sandor, however, seemed really taken with the topic. "Once you get used to all this," he told Gordon, "you could take some night courses. You don't have to give up your education."

In the rearview mirror, Cole saw Gordon open his mouth, then shut it. It looked to Cole as if Gordon would like more college about as much as he would like to swallow more beer.

"You should stay with premed," Sandor added. "Work

hard, get good grades. You could study this question of whether we die and then tell Cole that he is wrong!"

Cole snorted.

"Why do you laugh like that? Of course we will die," Sandor informed Cole. "It's part of the cycle of life."

"We are *not* part of the cycle of life."

"Don't be silly. If nothing else, one day the sun will explode and the earth will be destroyed along with it. We'll *have* to die then, won't we?"

"I wouldn't count on it."

"Look at it this way," Sandor said. "What if, like Harold, your head got cut off? How could you live with your body unable to receive any messages from your brain? And what if a train fell out of the sky and crushed you flat as a pancake? Of course you would be dead."

"Unconscious, maybe."

"When I was a boy in Boravia, you know what they did to the *strigoi*? First they dug them up. Then they cut off their heads, which they threw into a river. And then they burned the bodies that were left. Now you tell me those people weren't dead! Of course, they were already dead to begin with, but if they hadn't been, I guarantee

146

they would have been by the end of the day!"

"If they were already dead," Gordon asked, "why did anyone dig them up?"

"Oh, those were the days when they thought plagues and such were caused by the *strigoi*, the *vlkodlaks*. So they dug the poor people out of their graves."

"Even if they weren't already dead," Cole said, "it wouldn't surprise me to learn that they just went into sort of a permanent hibernation."

"With their bodies burned up! You mean just the heads?"

"Yes. Think about it, Sandor. What happens when we die the first time?"

"Oh, we don't really die then, Cole. Not completely. Our hearts and lungs take a little break, but they start again before our brains are affected. It's just a pause. There is no such thing as a permanent hibernation. Every living thing must give and take—air, water, nutrition—you name it. Everything must interact with its environment. That's being alive, by definition."

"What if a living thing could go a long time between giving and taking—like, say, centuries? Millennia?"

"Cole, it is a very good thing you have us with you.

You come up with such strange ideas on your own."

"Just because you don't agree with an idea doesn't mean it's strange."

"In any case," Sandor said, turning to Gordon, "I thought you did very well tonight. Wouldn't you agree, Cole?"

The evening *had* been encouraging. And it did seem that the kid had only needed some structure and a firm hand.

But it was still too early for unqualified praise.

"Except for the pawing," Cole answered. "Except for the ogling and the major breach of etiquette."

Gordon had been leaning forward, listening to Sandor's tale of dug-up *strigoi*. Now, in the mirror, Cole saw him sit back—whether thoughtful or stung Cole could not tell.

Either was fine with Cole.

CHAPTER TWELVE

GORDON seemed to be catching on. Each of the next few nights, he fed on his own after a couple of attempts, with only one try fumbled badly enough to make the omni screech. It was more than Cole had hoped for—he'd figured that he and Sandor would have to get a feed started for the kid fairly often at first.

"Anyone want to scout out locations for tomorrow's feed?" Sandor asked as they wheeled their suitcases down a carpeted motel hallway. "I saw a nice-looking place down the street that might—oh, never mind. I can see that you're both tired. We'll just stay in and watch TV then. Gordon, how about that?"

"Fine with me," Gordon said.

"Me too," Cole agreed. He *was* tired. Tired of being

responsible. Tired of playing bad cop. And very, *very* tired of lecturing. Except for an occasional put-upon sigh from Gordon, neither he nor Sandor seemed to be bothered by it; but Cole was sick of the sound of his own voice.

However, lecturing was what he was here to do. "Notice that we try to stay in a hotel with an inside hallway," he told Gordon, as their suitcases whined along the carpet. "If there's a choice, you don't want a room that can be entered from the outside, because maids have been known to ignore the Do Not Disturb sign—and when they open the door, in comes the sun. Okay, here you are. One forty-five. I'm in one forty-seven." He stopped outside their door, wanting to make sure they went in.

"Cole, why don't you come over in a moment, and we'll play a game or something. Does this hotel have video games in the rooms?"

"I don't think so."

"Nevertheless, you will come over anyway?"

To his surprise, Cole found that he wasn't averse to the idea. He'd forgotten that he enjoyed being with some of the other hemes, especially Sandor. Forgotten that it was actually amusing to argue and debate with someone who took a strong position but never got angry or offended about being disagreed with.

Being alone wasn't something he'd undertaken on purpose. Somehow it had just seemed to come about gradually over the decades. The others liked to settle down for weeks or months at a time and Cole didn't, for the most part.

The truth was, he'd gotten into the habit of spending hours watching the road roll toward him, disappearing endlessly under the front wheels, while he thought about other things. He hardly even noticed the landscape anymore: Sometimes there were dark mountains looming outside the car windows, sometimes stars stretching down to meet open plain, sometimes lights from suburbs or squares of farmland under the moon. It all ran together into a blur.

Not for Sandor. Even just driving along a few nights ago, Cole had already zoned out when Sandor exclaimed, "Oh, I love this part of the state!"

Cole had blinked, looked around at the trees pressing up against the sides of the highway. It took him a moment to realize that Sandor meant New Jersey and that yes, this *was* an attractive spot, especially compared to the more utilitarian area where he'd parked his car while in the city.

"Will you come?" Sandor asked again.

"I was planning on being off duty for the rest of the evening."

"Then for the rest of the evening," Sandor said, straight-faced, "I give you permission to be as uninformative and uninstructive as you wish."

"All right, then—"

"I swear to you: If you say something even slightly edifying, I shall cover Gordon's ears so that he cannot hear."

"Okay, Sandor. I'll be there as—"

"And if you forget yourself and we *accidentally* find ourselves in the midst of an educational moment, I'll leap up and start singing Boravian folk songs to drown you out. Ah, look, Gordon. That is the first nonfeeding smile you will have seen from Cole thus far. Charming, isn't it? I promise; he will loosen up more and more as your progress wins his approval."

"Right," Gordon said. "Well, if it helps, I promise that I won't learn a thing."

Cole looked sharply at him. The kid had cracked a smile. He was joking.

Come to think of it, that was the first nonfeeding smile he'd seen from Gordon, as well. Still nothing like his brother Guerdon's quick flash of a grin, Cole knew, although precisely what that grin looked like he couldn't recall. He could only remember the essence, the *feeling* of it.

"I'll come over in a minute," Cole told Sandor and Gordon. He waited to see them safely into their room before going into his. As he unpacked, he let himself think about Guerdon a little bit. He remembered some of the events of his childhood, but mostly as something in a story, blurred and wrapped away under layers of years.

One crystal clear picture he had was of the long night after Guerdon's death—of watching over the body with his mother and sisters and the neighbors.

The women would dip the cloth in cool water with soda and, wringing it, lay it over Guerdon's face to keep away the flies. *This* Cole remembered, because of the intensity with which he had watched the clinging wet cloth make a featureless mask of his brother's face.

He'd been eleven or so, a year older than Guerdon; and he'd sat rigidly upright, unmoving, waiting and hoping to see the cloth rise or collapse when Guerdon started breathing again.

That was neither here nor there though.

Anyway, Gordon's hadn't even been a real smile, now that he thought about it. More like a half smile. Almost reaching the eyes but not quite.

A little bit later, when Cole walked into Sandor and Gordon's room—a mirror image of his own—Sandor had moved the desklike table over to the bed and pulled the hard-backed chair up to one side. Gordon was seated on the bed on the other side.

Sandor sat down in the chair. "Look, I have my cards," he told Cole, holding up a deck. "Shall we play gin rummy?"

"Gin is for two players," Cole told him.

"Not when I play. When I play, it is for as many people as I want." There was a hotel pad and pen on the table in front of him. Sandor picked up the pen and wrote three names at the top of the first page.

But Cole was feeling restless now. He wasn't ready to

settle into a game of cards just yet. "It's a little hot in here, isn't it?" he asked.

"Set the temperature anywhere you want," Sandor said. "Then come sit down." Cole walked over to the thermostat and adjusted it down a few degrees. He didn't go to sit down but wandered over to the window.

"What city did you say this is?" Sandor asked Cole, shuffling the cards.

Cole pulled the curtain aside and looked out. "Harrisburg," he said. Below, gated amid concrete, there was a hotel swimming pool. It was dark, the lights off. He liked swimming; it was one of the few things he truly enjoyed and looked forward to.

"Pennsylvania?" Sandor was asking.

"Uh-huh." That's what he wanted to do tonight. He wanted to go swimming.

"That is one thing about being on the road, Gordon," Sandor informed him, shuffling the cards. "Places run together in your mind. When you are able to be more independent, you can stay somewhere for years at a time if you wish. Then you can remember where you are."

"Will we be staying anywhere more than one night on this trip?"

"Yes," said Sandor. "Soon. You're doing very well, Gordon, you know."

Cole did not agree, not out loud. Didn't want the kid to get cocky.

He leaned one shoulder against the wall, focused on the pool area. "Don't deal me in just yet," he told Sandor.

"Yes, you must brood at the window first, of course. Cole is one of those brooding hemes," Sandor said to Gordon as he dealt the cards: *slap slap slap*. "In spite of it, he's good company. But as I was about to say: Sometimes I remember a place if there's something interesting about it. For example, if it's the Pumpkin Capital of the Midwest. Or there's some kind of road-side attraction, like . . . What was the name of that place with the swimming pig?" he asked Cole.

"I can't remember."

"A swimming what?" Gordon asked.

"Pig," Sandor said, picking up his cards and spreading them into a fan. "His name was Ralph. Are we playing for money? Not yet, perhaps? Here, I'll go first. Anyway, Ralph the Swimming Pig is what it said on the billboard. But we never got to see him."

Cole looked at them over his shoulder. Sandor would

win, he knew. Gordon *didn't* know it though; the boy frowned at his hand, planning his strategy.

"I didn't know you wanted to see the pig," Cole told Sandor.

"I didn't then. But now I think maybe I wish we had. When will we again get the opportunity to see a swimming pig?"

"It was somewhere in south Texas. Next time we're down that way we can keep an eye out for it."

"It's been so long," Sandor said. "The pig is probably dead. But," he said, brightening, "maybe he's like Shamu, and they merely bring in a new swimming pig and call him Ralph as well."

No one answered. The slap of cards was the only sound. Cole watched them: Gordon's brow beginning to furrow in concentration, Sandor seemingly inattentive. "It's worse now, with the days so long," Sandor said, glancing at the clock on the bedside table. "So many fun places are closed by the time it's dark. In the winter there's more to do."

"What about bars?" Gordon asked.

"Bars get boring very fast, my friend."

"I guess so, if you can't drink."

Instead of replying, Sandor laid his cards out on the table with a flourish. "Gin."

"Already?" Gordon peered at his hand, then at Sandor's, on the table. After a reluctant moment, he laid down his own cards, spreading them out.

Sandor began to add them up. "I started with a good hand," he said vaguely.

"Don't believe him, Gordon," Cole said. "And never, ever play poker with him."

"Forty-one, forty-two. I get forty-two; does that seem right to you?" Sandor didn't wait for an answer but wrote down the number. "Cole, are you ready to play yet?"

"No."

Sandor started shuffling again.

"Sandor," Gordon asked, "how come sometimes you have an accent and sometimes you don't?"

"Hmm. Very observant of you, Gordon. Sometimes it's wiser to appear to be from nowhere. But when I am free, when I am among friends, I choose not to lose sight of where I came from. Cole, now, Cole dropped his heritage as soon as humanly possible. Oh ho, you know it's true, Cole! Gordon, Cole used to say things like, *By hokey day*, and let me see, there was *varmint* and *crit-ter*, and of course there was my favorite, *I'll be jig-gered*." Sandor began to deal the cards. "I feel it was a terrible shame to let such a descriptive dialect slip away."

"It didn't slip away," Cole told him. "You can still hear some of it down South."

"Where it is dying in this age of satellite dishes and worldwide webs."

"Dialects are living things, Sandor. They evolve; they die. That's the way it goes."

"Not as long as I am here to keep them alive. It's like you and your photos. Did you know Cole is a photographer, Gordon?"

"No."

"Count your cards and make sure you have ten. Not only does he take photos, but Cole used to draw, too. And he painted when he had the chance. There was a time we traveled together, as we are doing now, and when we stayed for a while in—Where was it, Cole?"

"South Carolina."

"Yes, in South Carolina, Cole painted."

"What did he paint?"

159

"You go first, Gordon, since you lost. He painted peo-ple mostly. Always omnis. He never painted me, that's for certain!"

"Why would I want to paint you, Sandor? I can look at you anytime I want."

"To capture a moment in time, of course. Isn't that what you do with your photos?"

"I don't really do that anymore."

"No? Now that you mention it, I haven't seen your camera, this trip. Are you back to your sketches?"

"No."

"I always thought drawing must be more fun than pointing a camera and pushing a button. Put a little of your own sweat into it."

"Well, if as you say the point is to capture a moment, then photos are going to be more accurate. A painting or drawing is always going to be distorted, because the image passes through the artist's eyes and hands."

"Distortion? I would call it *style*. It's what gives the whole thing *feeling*."

"In any case," Cole said, "I think I'm going to bow out of any card games for now. There's a pool here, and I'm going for a swim."

He thought Sandor would make some comment about Ralph the pig, but Sandor just looked up at him, amused. "Why, Cole, I am shocked at you," he said. "It's two in the morning. You know the pool must be closed."

"I don't care."

"Take note, Gordon. The end of the world must be near if Cole deliberately intends to flout a rule."

"They don't even know, if you're quiet," Cole pointed out.

"If he ever decides to go skinny-dipping, then we will know that the apocalypse is upon us. Anyway, I have something regrettable to tell you," Sandor said to Gordon.

"Aw, no."

"Yes. Gin."

Cole eased into the pool area, holding the metal gate so that it wouldn't clang and announce his presence. He sat on a plastic chair and pulled off his sneakers. He'd already changed in his room, already had a white hotel towel. When he took off his T-shirt in one quick, practiced movement, he felt as if he were shedding the last of a binding skin.

Of course, he could not dive. That would make noise. He sat on the side of the pool and slipped quietly into the water. His one vice: swimming in hotel pools at night. When they caught you, they didn't do anything—only reminded you that you weren't supposed to be there. The only times he had been caught were when omnis had come in after him—usually noisy, splashing, sometimes drunk. Then the other guests called the desk to complain. But when Cole was alone, he was silent, and mostly underwater. He liked the eerie cool feeling of floating in another atmosphere.

Sometimes he wondered what would happen if he just *stayed* under the water, if he stayed past the point where he could hold his breath. What would it feel like to run out of air, lose consciousness? He knew he could not die, but he was curious how it would feel to drown. Probably it would hurt. It would certainly be very intense. He'd read a description once of what happened, second by second, when a person drowned. It sounded as if it would be frightening and painful, until your brain started shutting down—and then, he thought, it might be peaceful. He wondered if someone like him—someone whose soul was permanently welded to his body—could have a near-death experience.

What would happen to his mind when he appeared to be dead? Were the thoughts of the hemes underground as empty as the expressions on their apparently dead faces? What lay behind eyes that were empty, like marbles?

No point in thinking about it. If he held his breath, all that would happen is that he'd pass out and lie on the bottom of the pool until someone found him and called an ambulance. Then there would be trouble.

Now, floating under the surface in nine feet of water, he kept his eyes open and looked at the darkness. Here, in the water, darkness had form and meaning. It was thick, you could touch it. When you waved your hand, you could feel it. Out in the air, in the real world, darkness was merely an absence of light.

His chest was growing tight. He did not test the edges of his breath-holding abilities. He kicked his way up, popping through the water's surface with a gasp.

Then he began, as soundlessly as possible, to swim laps. It felt good after the hours behind the wheel.

He couldn't have said how late it was when he finally eased himself out of the water. He didn't towel off but sat in a plastic chair to drip-dry in the cool air, tilting his head back to look at the stars. It was as Sandor had said: The stars in the city had to fight to be seen. The few he could make out now were faded and weak. Still, it was all good—the silence, the air chilling his wet skin.

He heard the faint clink of the gate behind him and turned to see Gordon slouching over, hands in pockets. "Hey," Gordon greeted him.

Cole nodded but said nothing. He did not ask the kid if he was here for a swim, because he obviously wasn't—he was still fully dressed, in his jeans. Most likely there was something on his mind, something he wanted to talk about. Probably something about himself. He was still almost omni, and that's what omnis did—they talked about themselves.

That was okay; the cocoonlike water, the labored trance and rhythmic breath of lap swimming had done their work, had unwound the restless feeling into nothingness. Listening to the boy would only take time—and time was the one thing Cole had in abundance.

He settled back in his chair and waited for the kid to work around to it.

"Is this what you do all the time?" Gordon asked, looking at the water, which still rippled slightly from Cole's presence. "I mean, go from hotel to hotel, room to room, night after night after night?"

"Pretty much."

"Doesn't it get . . . old?"

"Yes. But there are worse things."

"Like what?"

"Getting complacent and decadent, like you would if you lived in the Building all the time. Or getting attached to an omni, if you stay too long in one place."

"Why is it bad to get attached to . . . to someone?"

"Because you have to leave them after a few years."

"Why?"

"Because you don't age and they do." Cole did not like this topic, but he knew Gordon couldn't tell. He sat perfectly still, hands resting on the plastic arms of the chair.

Thankfully, Gordon changed the subject. "Sandor sure does like to talk," he remarked, sitting on the end of the lounge next to Cole. "He goes off on all these tangents."

"Yes," Cole agreed, "but notice that while he was

going off on those tangents, he was also beating you at gin."

Gordon nodded. He sat quietly, looking out, not at the water, but at the parking lot.

"Something's on your mind, Gordon," Cole said—patiently, he thought. "What is it?"

"Um. Okay. We're going to be moving around for a while, right?"

"Yes."

"Any chance we'll be passing through Missouri?"

"Not really."

"But it's possible?"

"Anything's possible. But I have no intention of taking you. I don't think it's wise."

"I know I can't call my family or anything. But I thought maybe I could just kind of see them. From far off. They wouldn't have to see *me*. I'd just like to know if everybody's—I mean, I kind of want to check on Jill," he added.

Jill must be the girlfriend he'd ripped up during his first feed.

It wasn't that Cole didn't feel for the kid. But this was part of that slippery slope, the one that a heme shouldn't allow himself to start down. "There wouldn't be any point in it," Cole told him. "Better to cut all ties with one swift stroke."

"Why?"

"It's just best," Cole said vaguely.

Then he reminded himself: He wasn't here to be vague. Vagueness was neither helpful nor instructive. Nor was it necessary. All the kid needed was information; he didn't need *or* want Cole's life story.

"It's too painful to see them," he admitted, his voice flat. "Because you know that they're going to fade and die." *And because it's too tempting to try to create a companion from someone you love.* He decided not to say that though—didn't want to put any ideas in the boy's head.

Gordon didn't nod, didn't indicate that he'd heard. Cole expected him to press the matter; but he didn't do that either. He sat staring out over the water.

"Your first time," Gordon said after a moment. "Your first feed ever. What was that like?"

Cole considered. Why did the kid want to know? "It's been a long time," he said carefully.

"I mean—mine didn't go so hot. It's kind of hard to—

I did some things . . . well, some things I never would've thought I could do. I just wondered if I was, you know. Weird. Or normal. Or what."

Okay, Gordon wanted some form of comparison. That was fair enough. Cole was sure Sandor had already told about his first time. "Well," he said, cautious, "it was . . . crude."

It had been embarrassing, too—and that was with Johnny walking him through it. He tried to think it out—how much was necessary to say. He didn't want to go into a lot of detail, didn't want to dive into a morass of old feelings and display them for the wide-eyed perusal of this kid. But it *was* pertinent. The basics, at least, were fair game.

Johnny had told him to stay put, he remembered that. And he had obeyed—he'd known something was terribly wrong inside him, but not quite what it was.

"I think it was probably more controlled than yours," he told Gordon.

The first time he'd felt the Thirst—he remembered that better than anything. Not an emotion, not hunger, not sexual need, but all three wrapped into one. Thirst was an ever-expanding hole.

He'd thought he was going insane. Weird thoughts grew in his brain, turning into pictures. Steak—he'd thought about raw steak dripping with juices, welling blood. The thoughts—the bloody pictures—had grown by the second, by leaps and bounds as he waited for Johnny. It probably hadn't been more than a couple of minutes before Johnny had returned with the woman, but Cole remembered he was stepping from one foot to the other like a runner before a race, desire battling with disgust, his hands clenching and unclenching as disgust wavered and began to sink under the rising tide.

He decided he wouldn't mention the Thirst to Gordon. After all, it was a given; Gordon already knew what Thirst was like. No need to bring it up.

"It was in the city, in an alley," he told Gordon. "Johnny brought me a woman. Most likely she was a prostitute. I don't know how else he could have gotten her to come back there."

He remembered Johnny's hand firm on his arm, the calm command of his voice. At the same time, a horrifying certainty that something was not right, something frightening and uncontrolled was swelling inside.

It had made him cling to the very edge of obedience to the only person who seemed to know what was happening.

"Johnny told me to hold on," he said to Gordon. "He told me to hold on just one more minute. Johnny said that control is everything."

He'd almost been dancing with wanting, and, he remembered, the whole inside of his mouth felt shriveled, his tongue like a dried-up snake, and his insides were empty and shriveling, too, just like his mouth. To add to his misery, his gums had begun to itch like mad.

Huh. He'd forgotten that, until this moment.

No point in mentioning *that* either.

"Johnny told me—very quickly, I remember—he told me what I had to do. He had some kind of tool. He pulled it out of his pocket. But it was dark, and I didn't know what it was."

It had been small—likely a nail, a tack, something like that. Something sharp.

And now Cole remembered something else: Johnny had run a hand through his hair. He'd been nervous—*Johnny* had been nervous!

He didn't tell Gordon that though. "I don't remember

what the woman looked like. Her dress, how old she was, anything."

He did remember that her dress had a scooped neckline. How he'd stared at that swooping curve that marked the boundary between cloth and skin! And when Johnny let go of his arm, without a word he'd grabbed her—before Johnny could get to her at all, before Johnny could get her started, Cole had pressed her back against the rough boards of the building. She'd laughed—he remembered that, she *laughed*—as he'd buried his face in her neck, above the curve of cloth, below the painfully sweet line of her jaw, driven by the wild urgency that he didn't understand.

"I fed from her," he told Gordon matter-of-factly.

The truth was, he'd found himself sucking desperately at her skin, rubbing his mouth on her, desperate for relief. That was the point at which she'd protested: *Hey*, she'd said, and tried to push him away.

But he couldn't let go. It wasn't like him to force himself on anyone, not for any reason; but his body was driven, goaded by a terrible need that he couldn't even identify. If she'd said anything, he could no longer hear it, even though he'd felt her begin to struggle in earnest, her hands scrabbling against his chest like little bird wings, as he sucked and licked and scrubbed his teeth and lips back and forth, almost sobbing with frustration, holding her tighter and tighter, her arms pinned against him. Later, he knew that Johnny had been there all along and that he had somehow gotten his hand in, just close enough for one quick jab on her neck with whatever he was holding—she jerked back with a little cry—and the barest thread of that rich, metallic scent quivered into Cole's nostrils. The puncture wasn't deep enough—Johnny had been lucky to get it anywhere on her neck at all—but now Cole found the source and latched on.

And then, then—oh, she'd gone completely still, and everything became wonderful. The salty tinge made him suck even harder, until it finally, mercifully turned into a thin trickle.

That was when he'd swallowed his first mouthful. It wasn't even a teaspoon's worth, but it was glorious. It was slick, rich, and he couldn't get it down fast enough. With his lips on her neck, she stood quiet with her hands suddenly soft against his chest.

He'd wanted to moan. Maybe he *had* moaned—he'd

never known for sure about that.

He mentioned none of this to Gordon. "And that was about it," he said. Clear. Concise. Simple.

"How did you know to stop?" Gordon asked.

"Johnny told me. He put a hand on my arm and told me to let go."

"That was it? That was all it took?"

Cole remembered that Sandor had said he'd had to hit Gordon several times to get him to let go. "He spoke very firmly."

That part of it was still foggy. Cole was pretty sure he remembered Johnny's voice in his ear; no words had sunk in, but he thought he recalled brusque syllables, the same tone you'd use with a horse that was carrying you too closely along the edge of a cliff. And, looking back, it now seemed likely that Johnny had hit him in the back of the knees, because he'd lost his balance suddenly and almost dropped the girl. *Then* he'd heard Johnny: *That's good, lad. Let her go now.* And Cole had obeyed, because the universe had gone upside down, and Johnny was the only solid thing in it.

"What about the lady?" Gordon asked.

"She never knew."

Aside from the feed, Cole had not touched her; nor had Johnny. Cole did not know what Johnny whispered to her or how much he paid her when she walked away.

Cole hadn't looked at Gordon at all while he talked; it took some work to dredge up this memory from under the layer of years, and even more work to separate the pertinent facts from all the feelings. But now, as Gordon said nothing, he turned to see that the boy's head was down, his face in shadow.

Cole could have let it go, he knew. But prying his own memories loose seemed to have loosened something else in him as well; he could *feel* the unhappiness that radiated from the kid almost in the same way the scent of chlorine now rose from his own skin, his own pores.

"What was your first time like?" Cole asked.

Gordon shook his head.

"You said it didn't go well," Cole remarked—not pressing exactly. Just putting it out there in case Gordon wanted to pick it up.

And finally, after a few more moments of silence, he did. "It was nothing like yours," Gordon said in a flat voice. "She was my girlfriend. I hurt her. I was like this animal, this sick animal." He kept his face turned away from Cole. "Listen. I—I have to tell you something."

Whatever it was, it seemed to stick in his throat.

"Go ahead," Cole said. "It's very difficult to surprise me, Gordon," he added. He wasn't trying to be encouraging. It was just a fact.

Gordon nodded, but it still took him a moment to find words. When he did, they all came out in a rush. "What I felt, that first time—I mean, I wasn't thinking about *killing* exactly, just wanting . . . you know. Blood. I was crazy for it. I didn't want to stop till I'd taken every drop she had. But that's the same thing as wanting to kill, isn't it?"

"It's not the same thing at all," Cole told him.

"No, no. You don't *get* it." Gordon raised his head to look directly at Cole. "I'm not like you. You're always cool and controlled. But I—" He hesitated, then went on in a rush. "You didn't see what I did to her. And I care about her! I—I *love* her, you know? But it didn't make any difference. I got going, and nothing else mattered. I'm sick." His voice was intense with self-hatred. "I'm a monster. I *liked* it, I *liked* doing that to her. And there's too many things—feeding makes me want too many things," he added, his shoulders slumping. "I don't want to be this way anymore."

"You aren't a monster," Cole said firmly. "What you

did to Jill—we all start off that way. Like animals."

"*You* didn't start off like an animal."

"I did. It's like you said, I got going and nothing else mattered. I wanted to keep going until I'd taken it all. *Exactly* like you said."

Gordon gave him a quizzical look.

"My first time was controlled, but only because Johnny was there all the way through. If I had been alone, I wouldn't have stopped. I remember that clearly: It wasn't enough. We all would have done the same thing you did. We're *all* one step away from being animals. Every time I feed, I want to keep going till I take it all. *Every single time.* And every time Sandor feeds, he feels the same." Cole leaned forward. "Gordon," he said, "what happened to Jill was not your fault. It was not in your control. Do you understand?"

Gordon nodded. He did understand, Cole saw. And he wanted to believe it. Cole wasn't sure the kid quite *did* believe it yet but hoped he was starting to.

"You had no idea what was happening to you," Cole went on. "*Now* you are beginning to understand. And you don't have to deal with it alone. Sandor and I are here, and our job is to keep you safe until you become familiar with your new limitations. Which, I might add, are the exact same limitations that the rest of us have."

Gordon was meeting his eyes now. Not a darting omni glance but the steady, penetrating gaze of a heme.

"You've already experienced your breaking point," Cole told him. "You know what it feels like. The object now—and for the rest of your life—is to never get to that point again. *Never*. To always stay in control." He waited a moment, but Gordon remained silent. "Any other questions?" Cole asked, sincerely hoping there were not. He didn't want to do any more explaining tonight.

"No. Just . . . thanks."

"For what?"

"For . . . I dunno. When I talk to Sandor, he tries to make everything sound upbeat and better than it is, so, you know, what am I supposed to believe? But you tell how things really are. It makes everything feel more . . . solid."

"Good," Cole said. "That's what I'm here for." He rose from his seat. "Shall we go in?"

"Sure."

They walked together back toward the hotel

entrance. "Hey, listen," Gordon said, as they approached the metal gate, "you guys should call me Gordo. That's what my friends call me."

To Cole it sounded like the label on a can of beans, but he didn't say so. "Gordo," he said, trying it out, and to his surprise it seemed to fit the kid.

"We're friends, right?" Gordo asked him. The heme was gone again, and the boy seemed bashful and needy.

No, they were not friends. Friendship implied equality. Cole was here to teach, Gordo to learn, Cole to give, Gordo to take. But he couldn't bring himself to deny it, to be so brutal as to throw the kid's overture back in his face. He just gave Gordo a brief smile, then lifted the latch and held the gate open.

As Gordo walked through, he gave Cole a grateful glance. He'd taken the small gesture to mean yes.

CHAPTER THIRTEEN

GORDO fed on the first try the next evening. Cole could tell he was pleased with himself—as was Sandor.

But Cole felt that any success at this point was mostly due to luck, not to intelligently applied skill. Something about the kid's attitude still hadn't quite clicked yet.

For one thing, on every single feeding attempt, Gordo had gone after young females exclusively. And if he said anything at all about his feeds, it was in terms of appearance: figure, weight, face, hair. He seemed to see hunting as a type of sexual conquest rather than an issue of nourishment and safety.

For another, the boy did not ask any questions about feeding techniques. He'd asked about the Colony or where certain people came from—and more than once he asked about heading toward Missouri—but never about anything to do with the process of getting blood out of an omni's body and into his own. He was brusque and impatient when Cole pressed him about any of the mechanical aspects of feeding.

To Cole, Gordo seemed to be tap dancing around the fact that he now got all his sustenance by latching onto other people's veins and arteries.

On top of that, the kid's packing techniques definitely left something to be desired.

Cole was the one who lifted the luggage out of the trunk when they stopped for the day at a motel just outside Philadelphia. As he picked up Gordo's suitcase, he immediately noticed that it had a strong smell of something like soap or shampoo. Cole handed it over to Gordo with distaste, certain that sloppy packing had taken its toll. And sure enough, once they checked in they discovered that Gordo hadn't put a cap on tight, or it had worked its way loose—in any case his clothes, which had been crammed in like so much tossed salad, were now coated with a slimy layer of Herbal Essences.

Sandor thought the mess was funny, and Gordo

merely held up bits of clothing, saying "Ew" and "Gross."

It wasn't that Cole minded having to take time for laundry, because he didn't. It wasn't that the suitcase was ruined, because it wasn't. It was just that he had the feeling he had missed something without meaning to. It might be a small thing, but he'd let the Ziploc situation slide one night too many, because—he had to admit it—bugging the kid about sealing his toiletries just seemed too much like nagging.

But that's what this trip was for: to teach Gordo the finer points of life on the road. And Gordo had a *lot* to learn; they hadn't even started on the more aggressive feeding methods, and of course Cole was holding off on the worst-case emergency procedures such as lock-bumping and picking pockets for keys or cash.

Gordo had a long way to go. Cole needed to pay attention and keep up with the details all the way through if he expected his teaching to have the proper outcome.

So he gave Gordo a quick reminder about proper packing, about double-checking the tightness of lids and his Ziploc seal. And early the next evening he found a Laundromat not far from the motel. It was in a tiny strip mall, with the Laundromat, a dentist's office, an electronics fix-it shop, and a bar.

"This is fortunate," Sandor said, as Cole fed dollar bills into the change machine. "We can go next door and feed while we're waiting for the clothes."

Cole wasn't at all sure that a place called The Poop Deck would be teeming with omnis, even if it was a Friday night. "You can't put that red shirt in with the rest of the load," he informed Gordo. "It'll turn all your whites pink."

"What do you mean?"

"Just what I said. Didn't you do any laundry at college?"

"No, I went *home* on weekends," Gordo said with a pointed look. "My *mom* washed my clothes for me."

Cole ignored the hint. "You should just get rid of that shirt. It's going to be a pain."

"I don't care," Gordo said, stubborn. "Jill gave it to me, and I'm keeping it."

The last quarter rang into the tray, and Cole scooped up the handful. "Then don't waste a whole load on it. Just wash it in the sink later," he said, walking over to put quarters in the slots. "You forgot the detergent," he said, as Gordo shut the lid on the filling washer.

"Okay, okay." Gordo picked up the tiny box and turned it around in his hands, trying to figure out how to open it.

"Pull the—"

"I see." Gordo sounded annoyed. But he ripped off the top and poured the soap into the machine.

"And now," said Sandor as Gordo shut the lid again, "shall we away to The Poop Deck?" Sandor thought the name was funny and had worked it into conversation four times already.

So they left Gordo's clothes agitating and started next door.

"Go put your shirt in the car," Cole told Gordo, handing him the keys.

Later, Cole reflected that this statement was the defining moment of the evening. His fault: He should have known that the kid needed an escort for a two-second drop-off.

He and Sandor walked on into The Poop Deck. The reason for its name was immediately apparent; the dark-painted walls had a nautical theme, being hung with oars, life rings, and ships' wheels. The clientele seemed to be mostly blue-collar types, meeting with friends after a hard week's work.

Sandor went straight to the bar to order. Booths lined the edges of the room; all the tables were in the middle. Cole chose a booth at the back.

Sandor was still at the bar when Gordo slid in opposite Cole, who did not bother to look around. He was already scouting for feeds and had singled out a group of middle-aged ladies in blue jeans. He didn't say this to Gordo though; he merely asked, "So, what do you think?" meaning that Gordo should look around for himself and suggest a possibility. He had been doing this for several nights, asking Gordo to consider the qualities that might make for a good feeding prospect, to verbalize them and weigh them against one another.

"What do I think about what?" Gordo asked. Then, as Cole gave him an exasperated glance, he added, with great pride, "I already fed."

Cole focused on him. "You what?"

"I already fed," Gordo repeated, triumphant. "Outside. Just now. Don't worry, dude," he said, seeing Cole brim over with disapproval, "I was totally smooth."

"Outside? In the *parking lot*?"

"No, on the sidewalk. That chick over there—see, the one that just walked up to that table? She didn't even know!" he added with glee, as Sandor came up with three tall glasses. "Hey, guess what, Sandor? I'm already finished for the evening. And I did it all by myself," he added, with another glance at Cole. "Just grabbed a girl and went for it. And you two haven't even—"

"You *grabbed* her," Cole repeated. "On a city sidewalk, you just grabbed someone."

"Nobody was around!"

Sandor eyed them both as he passed out the drinks. He sat down next to Gordo.

"Nobody?" Cole asked. "There were no cars passing? No one in a parked car? No one across the street? No one looking out a window?"

"I didn't see anyone."

"You are treating this too lightly!"

"I'm sure it's fine, Cole," Sandor said. "No harm done."

"He is *not* ready to—to . . ." Over Sandor's shoulder, at the front of the bar, Cole saw someone come in the door, and his voice died off.

It wasn't an omni at all. It was a heme Cole had never seen before.

CHAPTER FOURTEEN

HE was pale, thin, rather small as he stood looking around the room. Blond hair, cut short . . . and black eyeliner—not good. Dressed too much like the Building omnis—that wasn't good either: black jeans, black leather jacket over a black shirt.

As Cole looked him over, he saw that the index finger of the heme's left hand was covered in shiny metal, the tip coming to a sharp point.

Good God.

A finger guard. Hinged at the joints, usually decorated with filigree or sculpted designs, it was worn solely by omnis who enjoyed playing at being "vampires."

Something was very wrong with this picture.

Cole had not moved; he sat perfectly still, but Sandor knew something was up. He kept his eyes on Cole and did not move either. Gordo didn't notice that anything was wrong; he stirred his straw around in his drink, still sulking at the rebuke.

Cole thought quickly. The heme *had* to be a stray—a heme who had been abandoned soon after creation. No sensible heme would use any tool so blatant as a decorative finger guard. No normal heme would dress in such a way.

He had no doubt that this heme had seen Gordo feeding outside and had followed him in. Strays were rare; it was terrible, terrible luck.

Cole's mind was working like crazy. He must not allow Gordo to interact with any stray. Not now. Gordo hadn't had a chance to develop a proper and secure view of his place in the world. Strays were not known for their tight grip on reality. Left to shift for themselves without guidance, they tended to build some pretty bizarre explanations for their own nature.

They also generally didn't last long aboveground.

"Do *not* turn around," Cole told Sandor quietly. "I think Gordo's attracted a stray."

Gordo looked up from his drink. "Don't move," Cole said.

Something in his voice or face must have showed his

tension. Gordo didn't ask why, but obeyed.

Sandor's attention was sharp on Cole's face. "You're kidding, I hope."

"This guy is dressed like Count Chocula."

"Are you sure it's not just one of those omni wannabes?"

Cole gave him a withering look. He'd met lots of wannabes. He'd have to be utterly stupid to mistake one for a real heme.

"All right, all right," said Sandor. "I'm sorry; of course you're right. But maybe he's just from somewhere else, some other country?"

"Transylvania, maybe. Crap, he's not doing anything; he's just leaning against the wall by the door staring at us. He's not even sure what we are."

"What's a stray?" Gordo asked.

"Shh. Not now." They could just leave, Cole thought, walk out and perhaps the stray would *never* know for sure what they were. But what if he followed them? Cole did not want any stray to know where he and Sandor and Gordo were staying. Not until he knew what the heme's mental state was.

Think, think. He had to keep Gordo safe—but he also

had a responsibility to the rest of the Colony. He ought to at least find out what kind of person this was. And, perhaps, who had created him?

Cole's hand was on his drink, and he kept his head turned toward Sandor—but his eyes watched the stray closely. The fellow had a look of age; he was not as new as, say, Gordo.

Maybe he *was* a weird sort of accident; maybe someone hadn't known that they'd killed. It was unlikely, but possible. The only alternative, as far as Cole could see, was that whoever created him had shirked their responsibility. Had just left him to make it or not on his own.

But who? No one in the Colony would do such a thing. It seemed even less likely than someone not knowing they had killed.

He decided. "I'm going to go over there and talk to him," he told Sandor. "I don't want him to approach us." He turned to Gordo. "But if he *does* end up over here, do *not* mention the Building at all. Say nothing about the Colony. As far as this guy knows, we're the only other hemes in the universe. Sandor will explain," he added quickly, seeing Gordo opening his mouth to ask more questions. "Just follow directions for now. Please."

He slid out of his booth and made his way toward the heme, who watched him approach. Cole could see the stray's puzzlement. He still wasn't sure whether Cole was a heme. He'd obviously *seen* Gordo feed, but he was still undecided!

And he was staring openly. He didn't even know enough to be wary.

Damn, damn, damn.

The heme tensed as he approached.

"May I have a word with you?" Cole said quietly.

The heme stared at him. His eyes were round and blue—they would appear innocent, even childlike, to an omni, but Cole saw the depth of years in them, as well as that piercing quality unique to hemes. And there was something else, too, something he couldn't quite put his finger on.

The stray inclined his head. "You may speak," he said, as if granting permission.

Cole made a deliberate sweeping glance around The Poop Deck. "This isn't a good place," he said.

The stray hesitated. Then he gave that odd little bow of his head again, an almost courtly gesture. "Would you care to accompany me to my lair?"

Cole felt a sudden desire to laugh. *Lair?* he thought, but he let his face show nothing. "Where?" he asked.

"Not far."

"How far?"

"Across the street." The heme raised one hand in a languid pointing gesture that was useless, because The Poop Deck had no windows.

Cole saw now that the guard on his index finger was a shining metal claw, clear up to the knuckle, that bore an animal head of some kind, a wolf or a boar. Cole had been right; the point was filed needle sharp.

He didn't agree to go to the "lair," and he didn't move. He'd met strays before, but it had been a while—the last one had been living off rats and squirrels and pigeons. The one before that was in . . . Las Vegas? Somewhere in Nevada—that one had set herself up as the goddess of a love dungeon.

He did not want to go to this guy's home. But he didn't want to talk to the stray here in plain view and within earshot of omnis. Nor did he want to take him any-where—he didn't want this heme to get into his car.

"I won't harm you," the heme said. "I don't foul my own nest."

So he didn't know that he *couldn't* harm Cole. But he knew enough not to feed where he slept.

That was promising, wasn't it?

And if he was managing to survive alone—that said something too.

But the look in his eyes—it was *off* somehow. Sly, or . . . or . . . something.

This was such a strange situation—and no time to think. No plan for this.

"You have nothing to fear," the heme added with a slight frown, "unless you're human. And you're not, are you?"

Of course I'm human, you nitwit, Cole thought. "Very well," he said. "Let me just tell my friends I'll be stepping out."

"They may come, too, if they wish."

"Thank you, no." He went back to where Sandor and Gordo were sitting. "I'm going to accompany our friend to his *lair*. He says it's across the street. Will you come to the door after a moment and make sure you see where we go?"

"Of course," Sandor said.

Cole nodded. "If I'm not back in forty-five minutes,

you might come looking."

Sandor checked his watch. "It's one thirty. I have to say," he added, "I'm rather hoping I'll get to see a *lair*. I never have before, you know."

"I'll tell you all about it," Cole said.

He returned to the heme, who turned without a word and walked out the door.

Cole followed. Now he must find out as much as he could, then choose what to do. He would have to decide: Should he offer this stray the option of meeting the others, of learning from them? Offer to take him to New York?

He had a sudden mental picture of the four of them making their way back to the East Coast in his car.

Two uncouth, untutored hemes in his care.

The thought made him feel sick.

The heme's "lair" was in an apartment building across the street—visible from The Poop Deck's front door, Cole was glad to see—a long two-story with lines of doors top and bottom like holes punched in a shoe box.

The lair itself was on the second floor, up a metal staircase—an efficiency with an ancient, muddy-colored carpet. The only furniture was a mattress with a brown sleeping bag heaped at its foot.

Poor and dirty—just like it used to be in the early years, before the Colony. Cole had spent too many days shivering in his sleep in places like this.

If the guy wasn't a total loony, it would be nice to show him that there were other ways to live.

Once inside, the heme removed his jacket with a flourish. "What's your name?" he asked, dropping the jacket onto the counter that opened into the kitchen area. At first glance an omni might think that his arms were a little thin, but Cole saw muscles flex under the skin and knew that they were absolutely toned and fit.

The stray slowly pulled off his finger guard. Cole noticed that the fingernail on his right thumb was filed to a point. Perfect for grabbing a throat and piercing its jugular.

"You can call me Zeke," Cole said. Just a precaution.

The heme did not introduce himself. "Where do you come from?" he demanded. He set his finger guard carefully on top of his jacket, but he never took his eyes off Cole.

"I'm a traveler." Cole kept his voice carefully neutral.

This guy obviously felt himself to be superior, and Cole was not about to disabuse him by demanding any answers of his own. Not yet, anyway. He would play the meek supplicant as much as possible. And he would lie through his teeth about anything to do with his current task. If lying turned out not to be necessary, he would clear it up later.

"How did you come to be a vampire?"

Cole didn't even blink at the word. "I was walking at night," he told the heme, taking Gordo's story as his own. "And somebody jumped on me, knocked me out. When I woke up, I was like this. May I ask, what is *your* name?" he added, as humbly as he could.

The heme did not answer. "And when did this happen to you?"

"A little over a month ago."

"Yes," the heme said with a slight look of disgust. "You still dress like a human. And what of your friends?"

"I created them," Cole said. "I did not mean to. I no longer feed to the death."

"So no one has taught you anything."

"No. I'm on my own."

The heme leaned back against the counter and folded his arms. No plopping down on the floor for this guy, Cole thought—that would be undignified. "You may call me Royal," he said, and gave a solemn nod in the direction of the mattress. The meaning was clear: Sit down.

Uh-huh, thought Cole. *At his feet.*

He lowered himself onto the mattress—not too close. A clear shot at the door, in case . . . what?

This guy was stronger than he seemed, Cole could tell—but Cole was strong, too.

And what could he do to Cole anyway? Nothing. Really, there was nothing to fear. It was just that the look in his eyes was a little creepy. A little . . . unhinged?

"I do not create others of our kind either," Royal said. "I take only what sustenance I need."

Cole nodded. That was good. He wanted to ask some questions now. He just hoped he could appear submissive while doing it. "May I ask," he said, "how *you* came to be?"

"I was chosen."

"By whom?"

"By the powers of darkness."

"Did the . . . powers of darkness go by any other names, by chance?"

Royal just stared haughtily down at him.

"Were they male? Female?"

Royal did not answer. Finally, Cole understood: This was a staring contest, and Royal wanted him to look away first.

So he did. He bowed his head and focused his gaze on Royal's feet. Black boots, of course, with black laces that had silver tips with some kind of design on them.

"The powers of darkness have no physical being," he heard Royal say. He didn't look up, and Royal added, "I am their master, *and* their servant."

Huh?

"You are the master of the powers of darkness, *and* their servant?" Cole repeated.

"That is correct."

"How do you serve them?" Cole asked. Still careful not to engage Royal's eyes, still careful to tinge his voice with respect.

"I offer them gifts."

"What kinds of gifts?"

"The lives of humans."

Oo-*kay*, Cole thought. "You kill?" he asked calmly, wanting to be sure.

"Yes. You don't?"

"I have." Cole didn't mention that he'd only done it once. "But I thought you said you don't feed to the death."

"I don't. Their behavior gets too erratic when they die like that. I prefer other methods."

Cole glanced up. Royal's eyes were gleaming.

Surely he was lying.

Cole must not miss a step. He must take care with every word. "What methods?" he asked, looking down at the carpet again. It was dark brown, and matted with age.

"There are many methods." Cole could feel how avidly Royal was watching him. Hoping for a reaction. "For example, if you put your fingers on their throats and press down, you can observe their faces as they die."

I won't be taking him back to New York, Cole decided.

Beyond that, though, he didn't know what to do. He'd only been talking to the guy for a few minutes. He shouldn't rush. Shouldn't take it at face value, *or* take it too lightly.

"Why do you want to watch them die?" he asked,

looking up again. His own face, he knew, showed nothing.

"When you have lived as long as I have, you will understand."

Cole didn't know what to say to that, so he just nodded.

Royal seemed to take the nod as a sign of interest, if not approval. "It's amazing," he went on, warming to his subject, "to watch the spark go out of them. The eyes go glassy of course, as if they can't see. But if you watch a few moments longer, the pupils will go, too. It's like two little black flowers blossoming. Just like little flowers," he repeated, almost to himself. "Here's what I think," he said in a confiding tone. "I think they're not really dead until the pupils dilate. That's one or two minutes between the time their body dies and the time they are really gone. And I wonder, What do they think during that time? *Can* they think? Can they hear? What do they see, inside their heads?"

Cole felt a chill. *What lay behind eyes that were empty, like marbles?*

He'd been wondering about hemes, though, not omnis. That was completely different.

"That's an interesting question," he said from the mattress. *Okay*, he was thinking, *Okay. I've got to go back and talk to Sandor*. And then he would call Johnny. Johnny would want to come out and see the situation for himself. Johnny would be able to tell whether this guy was for real or not.

In any case, this would be resolved within a few days at most. All he had to do was disengage, and leave on good terms.

"I speak to them sometimes, very softly," Royal was saying. "I ask them what they see. Of course, no one's answered yet. I wonder if they see a tunnel of light. I wonder what they feel. Do they have souls? What do you think?"

"I don't know."

"I think perhaps they *don't*. When the spark goes out of their eyes, they go out, too, like a candle flame. Yes, like a candle flame." He seemed pleased with his own turn of phrase. "But then, when I think about those moments right before their eyes turn into little flowers, I wonder. I do *wonder* about those moments between. My," he added with a laugh, "I am talkative, aren't I? I think it's because the same thoughts have been banging around in my brain for so long, with no one to under-stand. And my thoughts are such *good* thoughts, such interesting ideas."

"Good," Cole agreed. "And interesting." He couldn't quite figure out *how* to leave. If this guy was telling the truth, maybe Cole shouldn't leave him at all.

If he was telling the truth.

"Listen, Royal," Cole said. "I have to say that I think it might be in your best interest not to kill om—humans."

"Why?"

Because I don't want you murdering people while the Colony decides what to do with you. "I was just thinking that perhaps we owe them a certain respect? After all, our lives are dependent on theirs."

"They die anyway," Royal pointed out. "A few years more, a few years less—it's all the same, isn't it? I *help* them. I give them a little intensity. I make them feel something. And it makes *me* feel something, to watch them. Why should I stop?"

Ethics aside, Cole thought, and added out loud, "If you're caught—"

"Oh, yes—if I'm caught. Do you think they'll try to kill me?" He seemed oddly excited by the idea.

Nuttier than a fruitcake. "You're bound to be pulled into the sunlight if they catch you," Cole pointed out.

"I'm afraid of sunlight," Royal said, looking even more excited. "I've battled the sun, you know. Have you?"

"No."

"Don't. It's quite painful; you wouldn't be able to bear it. You would probably turn to ashes and blow away. That's what happens in the movies—but then, the movies exaggerate so many things. Reflections, for example—can you see yourself in a mirror?"

"Yes," Cole told him.

"So can I. And—have you ever turned yourself into a bat?"

"No."

Royal nodded, looking pleased that Cole had not surpassed him in bat-changing abilities. Cole could see that he was using this opportunity to measure himself, to test the opinion he'd formed about his place in the world.

That opinion was a bit *elevated*, to say the least.

"I'm sure I'll be terribly afraid if I am forced into sunlight." Royal was no longer looking at Cole; his eyes had an intense, almost blind expression—similar, Cole realized, to the look omnis had during moments of sexual pleasure. "I'll scream, too, I warrant. Can you imagine feeling something so intensely that it makes you scream? I'll certainly feel something then. Oh, I know what you're thinking, Zeke." He focused on Cole again. "You're thinking that if you drive a stake into my heart, I'll feel something. You're right, of course. Oh, don't deny it; I see it in your face. I knew I was courting danger by bringing you here. After all, we are in competition for the same prey, are we not? But when you get to be my age, you'll have learned a few things. You'll have learned that it all fades into one big blur. You'll have to struggle to keep from being dead inside. There will come a point at which you have to make yourself *feel*."

Cole had a sudden vision of himself flipping through his photos.

Or floating in the pool, wondering what it would be like to drown.

Stop it. This guy is trying to shake you.

"You either become a blur," Royal informed him, "or you make a game of it; you walk a tightrope on the edge of oblivion. That's the choice. And I can tell you that walking the tightrope is *delicious*."

You're nothing like this guy, Cole told himself.

"Do *you* have a soul, Zeke?" Royal asked, looking straight at Cole.

Did he? How could he? Whatever was alive about him had been sealed to every cell and neuron, entwined and absorbed so that it would never be freed.

It was an effort, but Cole did not look away. "I don't know," he answered.

"Do you think *your* eyes will turn into little flowers?"

Was it a threat? Or a game, a cat-and-mouse game? Was Royal crazy? Or posturing?

A struggle to keep from being dead inside.

Talk to Sandor—*that's* what Cole had decided to do next. Not sit here listening to this guy jabber. Cole would have to call Johnny—but first he must go back to Sandor.

Cole stood up, the mattress giving under his feet. "My friends will be expecting me. But I see that I have much to learn," he added carefully. "I'd like to come back in a little while, if I may. Will you wait here for me?"

"You don't have to go at all, Zeke. You can stay with me if you want. Your friends must be quite a burden to you."

Now that Cole was standing, he felt more in control. "I'm sorry, I can't leave them."

Royal considered. "Very well. You may bring them, if you want."

Cole wondered for a crazy split second whether he ought to bow and back his way out of the apartment. No. Even Royal might see the insincerity in that.

So he turned and walked across the room, listening for the sound of sudden movement, every muscle tensed for the feel of a hand on his back or shoulder.

But Royal did not follow.

As Cole reached for the doorknob, he looked back to see the blue eyes regarding him. He'd never imagined that eyes that color could look so flat and frigid.

"I shall await you," Royal said, again giving that regal nod.

Cole nodded back, but said nothing as he stepped out onto the concrete landing. He pulled the door shut, and when he heard it click, that was one barrier between them.

The stairs were another.

The cars in the parking lot were a third.

He didn't realize he'd been holding his breath until it all came out in a heavy sigh.

The Poop Deck's sign glowed red and white. He checked his watch. He'd been with Royal for less than thirty minutes.

CHAPTER FIFTEEN

"I learned exactly nothing," Cole told Sandor. They spoke in low voices, even though they were outside, standing by Cole's car in front of the Laundromat, having left The Poop Deck behind. Each watched the apartment building across the street; but Cole also kept glancing behind him, where Gordo was alone inside the Laundromat, shoveling his wet laundry into the dryer. Not that anything was likely to go wrong in a Laundromat. It was just that Cole felt he had to keep an eye on his charge.

But he did not want Gordo to hear this conversation either, and that's why they were standing outside. "My initial reaction," he told Sandor, "is that this guy represents a danger, at least to omnis. But I may just have been creeped out."

"If *you* were creeped out, that says something about the situation."

"But he *wanted* me to be creeped out. That was his intention. I'm betting it threw him off to learn that there were other hemes around. I think at least part of it was an act. But," Cole added, "it disturbs me to think there's a possibility he may really be doing the things he said. I made a mistake. I should have figured out something to do with Gordo so that you could come with me. You barely even got to see the guy. "

"I saw the finger guard though. Loved the finger guard."

It took a great deal to faze Sandor. His perpetual good humor was like an anchor. If Sandor had been with him, Cole realized now, he likely wouldn't have gotten rattled. "I want to get your take on him," he told Sandor.

"I can't wait to see his *lair*."

"It's on a par with the places we used to stay, back in the old days," Cole told Sandor. "Remember the flophouses?"

"Easy feeds," Sandor commented.

"Yes. But the flophouses were full of people. Royal lives alone." Was that good or bad, Cole wondered.

"So our little friend likes killing," Sandor mused.

"He *said* so. Whether he actually does what he says is another matter."

"I'm leaning toward no," Sandor said. "It seems unlikely that he could go around leaving a trail of dead bodies behind him without getting caught."

Cole had to agree, now, standing out here. It didn't make sense that a stray could survive with that kind of behavior. Cole had been thrown, too, caught off guard by some of the things the stray had said. He'd let it get to him. Hadn't used his head.

"Let's hope he's just . . . theatrical," Sandor added.

"He *is* that," Cole said.

After some discussion, they decided it wasn't wise to leave Gordo behind at the Laundromat. They'd drive over to Royal's apartment, park in view of the front door, and make Gordo wait in the car. Cole and Sandor would enter the apartment together.

"Um. Should I be worried?" Gordo asked as Cole pulled up to the apartment building.

"No," Cole told Gordo. "Just be cautious."

"About what?" Gordo leaned forward. "Does this guy have like, *powers* or something?"

He was quite in earnest. Cole heard Sandor bite back a snort of laughter.

"Of course not," Cole said in disgust. "Nobody has 'powers.' Jesus. Just stay in the car, all right? And lock the doors behind us," he added, as he got out of the car.

He and Sandor went up the metal stairs. At the top Cole led the way along the concrete balcony, stopping at the entrance to the lair.

The apartment door wasn't latched. It wasn't even shut, but stood a few inches ajar.

He and Sandor exchanged a glance. Cole knocked softly on the jamb. There was no response from inside.

"You sure this is the right apartment?" Sandor asked.

"Number twenty-four." Cole waited another moment, then pushed the door slowly open.

The mattress was there, but the sleeping bag was gone.

They walked in. Sandor looked around at the bare floors and walls, the empty counters visible in the kitchen. "Do you think you scared him off?"

Cole didn't answer. He went to check the bathroom. No toiletries, no towels. Not even a shower curtain.

He came back out. He said nothing, just shook his head: *No sign*.

"I believe our little friend has scampered," Sandor said.

"Let's wait in the car for a while," Cole told him, "see if he comes back. Maybe he just went to feed or something. The sun doesn't rise for another three or four hours."

"And if he doesn't show?"

"We should check back again tomorrow, just in case."

"What about *our* feeds?"

"Gordo already fed. It won't hurt you and me to skip a night."

They left the front door ajar, just the way it had been, and went back down the stairs. "What did you *do* to the little fellow, Cole?" Sandor asked.

"Nothing. I didn't do a thing."

"I think you frightened him. Maybe he's shy."

Maybe he's crazy, Cole thought.

They waited in the car. Around three thirty, Sandor walked Gordo over to collect his clothes. An hour or so before dawn, Cole went up and checked the apartment one last time. Still empty.

When he was alone in his hotel room, Cole called Johnny. He described the stray, gave his impressions, and repeated their conversation as best he could. "I'll check the apartment again on the way out tomorrow," he told Johnny, "just to make sure."

Johnny had listened intently, making no comments, but now he said, "Was the door unlocked when he first took you to the apartment?"

"No, he unlocked it."

"With a key?"

"Yes."

"And you said he had a mattress, and left it behind?"

It seemed rather an odd thing to focus on. "Yes."

"How big was it?"

"Twin size."

"What was it made of?"

"It was . . . I don't know. It was just a mattress from a bed."

"So it couldn't be rolled up and carried with him. And there was no other furniture?"

"No, just the mattress and the sleeping bag. Why?"

"I'm just trying to figure out how he gets around. He travels light—sounds like he could easily be on foot. But he had a key—so it's likely he was paying rent."

"Maybe he stole the key."

"Maybe. That's quite a risk, to squat in someone else's apartment. Even if it was unoccupied, it could easily *get* occupied at any time. Anyway, I'm thinking that if that's really his home base, and he's on foot, he may come back. But if he has a car, he's mobile. And he could be anywhere by now."

"Do you want us to head back to New York so we can discuss it with the group?" Cole asked.

"I don't see any point. There's *not* really anything to discuss right now. Nothing to make any decisions about. The only thing we can do is look around online to see if we can find any mention of him. Of things he might have done. You just keep on with Gordon."

"Gordo."

"What?"

"He likes to be called Gordo."

"Oh. Okay. Anyway, I'll let you know if we find anything. Royal sounds like a right crackpot."

"He was . . . weird."

"They all are," Johnny said. "But this one may be functioning in society, at least enough to have an apartment."

"I suppose." The apartment had looked barely functional to Cole. More like a roof over the guy's head than a home.

No wait, it was a *lair*.

"If he's there tomorrow," Johnny went on, "try not to scare him off. I want to talk to him myself."

"All right," said Cole.

"And if you don't mind, I'd like you to check back and let me know either way."

"I will."

"Talk to you tomorrow then."

"Yes . . . but listen, I wanted to ask you something," Cole said, then hesitated. "Well . . . never mind."

"No, go ahead," said Johnny.

"Do you think we have souls?"

Silence. It *was* an odd question to ask out of the blue, Cole knew.

He wished he hadn't brought it up right now. This was a subject more suited to leisurely evenings on the patio at the Building.

"I think it's a moot point," Johnny said after another moment.

"I know it is. We can talk about it another time." Later, in New York—where it was likely to turn into a long philosophical debate.

But Johnny continued. "For us, what we have here is all we're ever going to have. That's why we maintain relationships with our fellow hemes. Otherwise there's no difference between *our* existence and that of, say, a tree or a rock. And," he added, "I have to say that if a short meeting with a stray could get you questioning *your* place in the world, it was a good job you kept him away from Gordon. Gordo," he corrected himself. "Anyway, call and let me know if he comes back or not."

"Yes," said Cole. "I'll call."

But the next evening the apartment was still empty.

Royal the stray was also a moot point.

CHAPTER SIXTEEN

GORDO seemed a little subdued after his sidewalk-feeding adventure and its aftermath.

But Cole also noticed that he didn't get rid of his red shirt.

The nights took on a definite rhythm: The three would get up, leave the hotel, then go immediately for a feed. After that the evening was free, and sometimes now they even stayed at a club for a while before driving on to the next town.

Cole finally felt secure enough in Gordo's ability to *not* attract attention that he had okayed spending two days in the same hotel in Pittsburgh. Now Sandor wanted to feed in Castile, a medium-sized town off the highway, and so they headed into Ohio. Cole had been this way many times before and didn't think anything about it till he saw a sign loom up in the dark:

OLYMPIA MALL
NEXT EXIT

It must be a new mall. He didn't remember seeing it the last time he'd been through here—which would have been what, a dozen years ago? Longer? He would have remembered it with a name like that.

Olympia, Ohio. The settlement of his boyhood was long gone, eaten up by growing towns; but the name remained.

"The college is coming up," Sandor reminded him. Sandor had urged them to wait to feed in Castile because, he said, wasn't Gordo ready to hold off a bit? And besides, it was a Saturday night and this was a party school, one of Sandor's favorites.

Cole held the wheel steady, but most of his attention was now on his surroundings. There was nothing recognizable in the asphalt and concrete rivers that made up the freeway and its ramps. Now he saw the mall itself off on the right; from here it seemed to be mostly parking lot, with skinny lampposts that looked like forlorn twigs bearing luminescent berries. The mall was still open; he could tell because there were plenty of cars sprinkled under the lights.

"Take the next exit," Sandor said. "Turn right, and you will come to the campus."

Cole obeyed. He eyed the mall as they circled the edge of it; he was looking for a creek that used to run somewhere along here. Why shouldn't he? This area used to be his home. And it had been so long since he'd even thought about it—of course he'd have a natural, impersonal curiosity.

There was no sign of the creek. He saw a drainage ditch, lined in concrete, but no creek. Along the road, domesticated little wisps of oak and elm were carefully arranged on the manicured lawns of restaurants and office buildings.

Perhaps, he thought, these trees were the great-great grandchildren of the wild forest that used to be here. Back then, he remembered, the trunks were so big that three or four people holding hands could not get their arms around one. So old and tough that an ax dulled after only a few blows.

The campus was only a few minutes away. "Turn here, turn here!" Sandor said, and Cole pulled the car onto a tree-lined avenue of large houses, each one bearing Greek letters over the door.

They heard the music first, a thumping, blaring haze of noise. Then they saw the barricades ahead, blocking off a side street. As Cole drove past slowly, they could see a mass of people milling around behind the barriers.

"Perfect, a street dance," Sandor said, delighted. "Looks like there's a theme: the forties maybe? Do I look all right?" he turned to ask Gordo, who was in his now-accustomed spot in the backseat.

"Um, yeah. You look fine."

"Great! Cole, if you keep going straight, there's sure to be a space somewhere down there."

"Is it okay if I drop you two off?" Cole asked.

"You're not going to come?" That was Gordo.

"I'd rather go off on my own just for a bit."

Sandor had been looking eagerly out the window, but now he turned to give Cole a sharp look. "You've forgotten how to jitterbug, haven't you?"

"Of course I remember how to jitterbug. I don't *want* to right now, that's all."

"Very well then, do as you wish. We will have a good time while you do your romance-novel-cover brooding. Let us out at that corner there."

Cole stopped the car. Gordo started to get out, but hesitated. "Where will you go?" he asked Cole.

"I saw a mall as we were coming in. I think I'll try that."

Sandor opened his door. "Hmf. Malls, is it? Aren't they a little more difficult than street dances?"

"They're different."

"All right. We'll meet you back at this corner then in a couple of hours?"

"Sure."

"Come on, Gordo," Sandor said, sliding out of the car. "Put on your dancing shoes! Metaphorically speaking, of course."

"Sandor," Cole called. "Keep a close eye on Gordo."

Sandor turned back, bending over so he could look Cole in the eye. "Don't worry. He will feed before I do. I promise to keep him safe." Straightening, he continued, "If you want, Gordo, I will show you some dance steps that will make any girl swoo—"

The car door slammed shut, and they were gone.

Alone, Cole headed back to the mall.

Inside, he walked slowly past the bright storefronts. He briefly thought of his camera, locked away in the trunk of his car—but only briefly. He had always worked strictly in black and white anyway, and the canned lights that angled over the displays lacked contrast and emotion.

Hard to believe that there used to be a forest here. It had been like walking underwater, among those trees. Quiet, because the age-sodden layers of leaves underfoot muffled all noise. Still, because the wind couldn't reach through the thick canopy overhead.

And dark. Every once in a while a shaft of light would stretch out a finger, as if blindly trying to touch him. But it couldn't find him, couldn't see him, for the trees.

He paused. There was a girl working in the window of a bed-and-bath store; she was arranging bottles of lotion or shampoo in a basket. There was a name tag pinned to her blouse, but he did not look to see what it said. When she saw him watching her through the window, she smiled, and he smiled back, as if he had nothing better to do than watch a salesgirl rearrange stock.

Then his vision shifted and he saw the glass between them, with his own shining reflection layered over her. Parts of his body seemed blurred and half dissolved into the background, but his eyes gleamed like marbles.

He turned and walked away.

The floor was featureless tile under his feet. When he was a child, he couldn't walk more than a few yards in any direction without being turned aside by a looming tree; any path he chose was forced to wind and twist, and he was never sure which direction he was going. None of the children strayed far from the paths in those early, early days.

In the food court, he got in line at the corn dog kiosk to buy a soft drink. He stared at the back of the man in front of him for a while before it occurred to him that he'd better focus on his purpose. He'd indulged himself a little, and it hadn't done any harm; but now it was time to attend to business.

He pulled his necklace out and let it dangle in plain sight.

"Can I help you?" the girl behind the counter asked when it was his turn. She had on a sort of baseball cap, but it was pink, and the bill stuck out about a foot from her head.

"Just a Coke," he told her.

"Two nineteen," said the girl, pushing a drink toward him.

"Thanks," he said, smiling at her without even thinking about it as he pulled out his wallet. She couldn't help but smile back, of course.

He paid, and she gave him his change. "Straw?" he asked.

"Oh. Gosh. Sorry." Flustered, she handed him one.

When he turned around he saw two teenage girls sitting at a table, watching him sideways, one from under dark lashes, the other openly; and when he let his smile loose again, the latter one giggled.

The dark-lashed one was prettier. But the giggling one would be easier. Tonight, he decided, he would take the easier one.

Sure enough, twenty minutes later he was seated next to the giggler, whose name turned out to be Emily. Her dark-lashed friend was buying a pretzel, and when she turned her back, Emily cast a quick glance at him.

"I like your necklace," she said, still smiling. "Are those nails?"

He hesitated, pretending he'd forgotten. "Oh. Yeah," he said, looking down to lift the cross from its place below the hollow of his throat. "It was a gift."

"Well, I like it."

"Thanks. Want me to tell you something about it?"

"Sure."

"It's a secret."

"O-kay." She laughed again, but was still leaning toward him, interested, so, still holding the cross, he drew close to whisper in her ear.

"This won't hurt," he told her softly, his mouth just below her ear; and then he pressed the end of the longest nail into her neck. She gave a little gasp, but his lips were already on the puncture, and now she was still, floating in that numb, glassy-eyed state.

He didn't drink his fill, of course. He fastened his mouth to her skin and swallowing the pulsing trickle, not even enough to slow her heart the tiniest bit before he released her and sat back, the wound sealing as soon as air touched it.

". . . and that's where I got it," he said, as if finishing his story.

Her eyes focused. "I'm sorry," she said, confused, "I think I . . . zoned out for a sec."

"That's okay. It wasn't a very exciting story." He liked the ones that did that; sometimes they tried to fake it and pretend they had heard everything he'd said. He preferred the honest ones.

The dark-lashed girl came back over with her pretzel, and the three of them spent the next thirty minutes walking around the mall, talking, while he took note of the girls' facial expressions, their gestures, the slang they used. He noticed it all and stored it carefully away; he might need it sometime.

In the end, Emily gave him her phone number and he said he'd call. He'd said it so often, it wasn't a lie anymore, just a meaningless pleasantry.

He went by a skater shop and bought a shirt without trying it on. Then he stopped by the bookstore. He didn't buy anything until he was on the way out and saw the sale table: 75 percent off.

Teach Yourself Manners.

The History of Weaving.

Over 10,000 Names and Their Meanings.

Curious, he picked up the last one.

The book had a cartoon stork on the cover. It was meant to help parents choose the names of their babies. He had seen books like these often, in passing, but had never really looked at one.

He bought the book—$3.87, with tax—before he left the mall.

Sandor wanted to spend a second night near the college, so they drove to a hotel not far from the sorority and fraternity houses. While they were in the car, Sandor took up the name book with great glee.

"'Sandor,'" he read, "'a variant form of Alexander.' Shall we take bets on what 'Alexander' means?" he asked Gordo over his shoulder, as he flipped through to the front of the book. "I'll bet you one dollar it means . . . 'great and noble man of stature.' What do you think?" Without waiting for an answer, he began reading again. "'Defender of men.' Oh, that's even better." He sounded delighted. "Defender of men. That's me, all right."

"Look up my name," Gordo said from the backseat.

"Hmm." Sandor found the page, ran one finger down it. Then he started laughing.

"What?" Gordo sat up, trying to see over the seat.

"'Gordon,'" Sandor read. "'From the Old English *gor* and *denn*, meaning "a dunghill."' Oh, that's priceless."

"Let me see that." Gordo's hand came over the seat, reaching.

"No, no." Sandor held the book away. "Let me read the rest of it. It says, 'may also be a form of . . . of . . .' Can you turn the light on for a moment, Cole?"

225

"No."

"...'Gordius, meaning "bold."' Oh, I like that," Sandor said. "Much better than 'dunghill.' 'Bold' is definitely the correct meaning of your name. Here, take a look."

He handed the book to Gordo, who started thumbing through it.

"'Cole,'" Gordo announced after a moment, "'from the Old English, meaning "black" or "dark."' Huh. I'm not sure that fits."

"Of course it does. Look at his hair, and his eyes," Sandor put in before Cole could say anything.

"I thought his eyes were sort of brown."

"When they're that dark of a brown, they can be called black. Now see, Cole, we want that Luxury Inn up there," Sandor said, pointing. "They have extra pillows in the closets. I like a place that provides extra pillows."

"I like thick towels," Gordo said.

"Yes, and an air conditioner that works. And of course Cole must have a pool."

"Only in summer," Cole pointed out. He headed toward the place Sandor had indicated. It didn't make any difference, he supposed, whether or not Gordo knew what most everybody else did: that Cole wasn't his original name.

In his room alone, Cole picked up the name book and opened it, flipping through.

Ezekiel. *God will strengthen.*

His parents wouldn't have known what it meant. They'd been illiterate.

He'd used that name for a long time, and sometimes Zeke. When those became so unusual as to stand out, he'd started using his mother's maiden name, Cole. It was perfect—a little name, Cole, harmless and light. It truly belonged to him too—that was important; he had never cared for the idea of plucking a name for himself out of the ether.

Now he wondered for the first time how his mother and father had come up with the name Ezekiel, and what it had meant to them. Had he been named after the Bible prophet? Or a long-gone relative? Or perhaps they had just liked the sound of it.

He flipped a few pages, looking for other names he knew.

Johnny. *Pet form of John.*

John. *From the Hebrew, meaning "God is merciful."
Also: Jon, Johannes, Joannes, Jochanan, Johanan,
Yochanan, Johon, Jehan, Jan,* and so on for a thick
paragraph: *Jean, Ivan, Hans, Janne, Giovanni, Jock,
Juan, Sean, Shawn, Ian, Jenkin, Jovan, Jack.*

Johnny had probably used most of those names; he'd
spent so many years in so many places that he wasn't
really from anywhere anymore so much as he was from
everywhere.

Cole hesitated, then started turning pages till he
reached the *L*s.

Lulie. *From the Middle English* lullen, *meaning "to
lull, to soothe."* That did sound like Ma, what Cole could
remember of her—humming, wordless, her heel planted
on the puncheon floor, toe rhythmic on the cradle
rocker while her hands were busy, always busy.

But Cole could not quite remember what they had
been busy *with*. If he reasoned it out, he could come up
with a lot of things: carding, spinning, darning, sewing,
shelling, kneading, plucking, stirring. But he couldn't
see any of it, couldn't remember what his mother's
hands had looked like, or what they had done. All he
knew was that they seldom had been still.

Ephraim. That was from the Bible, he knew, but according to this book it meant "fruitful." True enough, Cole supposed. Pa'd had eight children before he died— but only four had lived past infancy.

Now he looked through the *G*s. Finally he found it— Guerdon.

Reward.

Now, holding the name book, he thought not about sitting up with Guerdon's body, nor the nightshirt Ma and Polly and Hannah had torn up to sew into his shroud, but about how out in the woods Cole and Guerdon had tried to cut off Guerdon's snake-bitten finger in an effort to keep him alive.

Guerdon was a year younger, but he knew as well as Cole what ought to be done. The two punctures were ugly red between the first and second knuckle, and the flesh had already started to swell. Both boys had skinned plenty of animals, but only Cole had his own knife. And besides, he was older. So he was the one to do it.

The knife was the clearest picture left in Cole's mind now. It had suddenly seemed so awful small when he pulled it from its sheath, the blade terribly short, and though it was sharp it sure wouldn't slice easily through bone. No, anybody who could cut off a finger with that knife would have to be both cool and fearless.

Cole had been neither; he could still see that moment like a snapshot—the moment the blade started trembling. He'd held it in the exact right place it needed to be, poised at the joint just above the palm—but at the moment it should have come down strong and firm, it instead hung in the air over Guerdy's familiar hand and began to quiver.

In the end, the knife had dropped nervelessly onto the ground and he had grabbed Guerdy and bolted for the cabin, a half mile away. Too far; and now Cole realized that the run back, with frightened, fast-pumping hearts, probably hadn't helped his brother any.

Huh. Now he remembered the feeling he'd had, looking up from those two punctures to see Guerdy's frightened face.

That's what it was; that's why Gordo had called his brother to mind. It wasn't anything about the kid in particular, nothing physical. It was his *need* that was the same. That was something neither Guerdon nor Gordo had been aware of but which Cole now saw clearly: a floundering need for someone to step in and be steady, to take charge and follow through and do what needed to be done.

Okay, so that mystery was solved. The bottom line was that Guerdon had died in the end, and all the woods were gone and his grave long erased by wind and weather, his bones turned to powder and lost under tons of concrete.

But Cole, who had gone off in the woods alone to cry till he puked, was still sitting here, and still in his eighteen-year-old prime. Cole had no doubt that he would now be able to cut off a poisoned finger without so much as blinking an eye.

Lucky for Gordo.

It was almost dawn. He smoothed the page with his fingers, thinking that he ought to go to bed.

Instead he turned the pages quickly, to look up his sisters.

Hannah. *Favor, or grace.*

Polly. *Variant form of Mary.*

All right, he thought, and turned to the *M*s.

Mary. *Derived from Miriam, meaning "sea of bitterness."*

That was Polly, all right. What he remembered most

about Polly was her nagging, wagging tongue. *Don't think you can sneak off and read your silly book while others do all the work. Not a crumb you'll get from this table so long as you shirk your share. Not a crumb, Ezekiel—you can starve, as far as I'm concerned.*

"Not likely," he said out loud, brushing Polly away with a flick of the pages.

Then he found himself turning the pages to look up another name.

Bess.

A pet form of Elizabeth. Of course; he knew that.

Elizabeth. *Oath of God.*

A mistake—a stupid, stupid mistake. There had been fear, he remembered that, how she'd trembled, white arms soft and clinging, how he'd guided her to the feed, full of power and control. The shame, the conceit of it.

But time eventually pressed all one's joys and sorrows into indistinguishable lumps. That was the good thing about time.

He shut the book and got ready for bed.

As he lay on his back, however, covers up to his neck, waiting for sleep to overtake him, another almost-forgotten memory came drifting into his head.

Probably brought up by the name book.

Polly's and Hannah's muffled giggles—that's what had woken him, tugged him out of sound sleep in a long-ago darkness, warm under quilts with Guerdon's soft snores uninterrupted beside him. How old had Cole been then? Five? Six? He did not move, did not make a sound, but peeked out, the air sharp and cold on his nose and cheeks. His sisters' white nightcaps and nightgowns were bright bobbing patches against the dark, long braids spilling over their shoulders. They stood in the moonlight that shone through the one small window their father had cut into the end wall of the loft, a kindness and a luxury that would let breezes through on sweltering summer nights. This night it had been fall, not summer, and the shutter shouldn't have been open; but Polly and Hannah needed the moon. Cole could see it framed in the window, visible through the black, shifting fingers of the mostly leafless trees.

He watched them taking turns looking over their shoulders into Ma's precious hand mirror. He did not know what they saw nor what they were looking for— just that they were doing some kind of fortune-telling. He could not hear what they said, only the quiet mur-

233

mur of their voices, the intermittent bursts of smothered giggles. And he remembered that when the shutter was back in its rightful place bolted tight against the night, and his sisters were finally safely back in their shared bed, he'd pulled the covers over his head against the frosty air, huddled closer to his brother's warm back, and drifted back into a warm quilted sleep.

There was nothing important in the memory. Nothing earth-shattering, nothing even particularly striking. Just a feeling that wasn't worth lingering over, because it was no longer possible: a feeling of contentment, and of safety taken for granted.

CHAPTER SEVENTEEN

THE next night, as usual, Cole went to collect Gordo and Sandor for the evening feed. The carpet muffled his steps; there was no sound. No outside light came into the hallway. It could have been midnight or noon. There was no way to know without a clock.

Through their door he could hear the tinny sound of the television and a low muted hum—that was Gordo's blow-dryer. Same as last night. And the night before.

He knocked on the door. Here he was again, he thought, retracing the same steps he'd carved out that first night the three of them were on the road. The same thing over and over again for days, weeks, months. The good thing for Gordo was that falling into a routine *was* second nature.

But this was Castile, Ohio, home of Sandor's favorite party school, and when Sandor opened the door, Cole saw immediately that he was dressed differently. He wasn't wearing jeans, not even khakis, but dark slacks, black shoes, a button-down shirt.

And a tie—it wasn't tied yet, but there it was, ends dangling down Sandor's chest. "Come in, come in," he said, holding the door open. And when Cole walked in, Sandor did not fling himself on the bed to watch the news but went to stand in front of the bureau mirror.

Cole stared as Sandor fastened the top button on his collar. "You two are on your own tonight, if you don't mind," he told Cole, looping the tie around and through itself in practiced movements. "I have a date."

Cole had not sat down. He stood by the armchair—this hotel had an armchair and no desk—speechless.

Gordo's blow-dryer hummed on and on. "A date for what?" Cole asked. Perhaps he had misunderstood.

"A date for taking someone out and talking and dancing and having a good time and whatever else that may lead to."

"A someone. What *kind* of someone?"

"This someone has brown hair. Nice body—"

"An omni." Cole squeezed his eyes shut. "Sandor. If you want to feed, just feed. If you want to have sex with somebody, just do it. But don't go on a date, for heaven's sake."

"Why not?"

"You're setting a bad example for Gordo."

"I don't agree. I'm just going to have a conversation with someone who is *not* one of us three. It will be a nice change."

"Omnis are not a nice change. They're dull."

"Again, I do not agree."

"Especially the young attractive ones. They have nothing to say, and they know it, so they try to let their bodies do the talking. And if you don't want them for sex, their bodies have absolutely nothing to say."

"Oh, Cole, that reminds me. You'll never guess what Gordo asked me last night. Out of the blue, mind you. He asked if I were gay."

"Oh. And you said?"

"I asked him whether he meant gay in the sense of 'merry,' or gay in the sense of 'enjoying sexual pleasure with men,' and he said the second one. So I told him that if he meant exclusively with men, then no, I'm not gay, but if he meant when the occasion arises, then yes, I am definitely gay."

"And what did he say?"

"Nothing. He just got an uncomfortable look about him."

"Charming."

"Yes, well, he's just a boy. Practically a baby. I told him that if in three hundred years he hasn't dipped a toe in the other end of the pond, to contact the newspapers because that will be a first."

"And he said?"

"Nothing. But he looked at me with so much mistrust I could not bear it, so I told him something. I said, 'Gordo, my friend, I think you're a nice fellow, but I expect to be acquainted with you for many centuries, and it would not be wise to risk bad feelings with one of the few people I am able to get attached to. So you need never hesitate to bend over and pick up the soap, so to speak.'"

In the bathroom, the blow-dryer stopped.

"Sandor—," Cole began.

"I would like to take the car, if that's all right. There are half a dozen places within walking distance for you two to feed. So taking the car isn't a problem, am I correct?"

"Yes, but—"

"Cole, life would be dull if we never did anything different. I refuse to be one monotonous note all the time: *bong, bong, bong.* I will be very careful with your car. And I'll be back before dawn. Ah, here comes Gordo."

Here came Gordo indeed, with his plastic bag of dirty clothes and his now neatly zipped Ziploc bag. For all the time he spent on his hair, to Cole it just looked like . . . hair, no different from Cole's own, which was towel-and-air-dried.

"Listen, Gordo," Sandor called to him as he walked over to his open suitcase. "After you two are back here, you should ask Cole to show you his photos. Some of them are really quite extraordinary." He turned to the mirror again and looked his reflection up and down. "Do I look all right?"

"You look fine. But Sandor, do you really think—"

"Cole, I really do. Now, don't wait up for me!" Sandor checked his wallet to make sure he had his key, and then with a bounding step, he was gone.

"He's sure happy," Gordo remarked wistfully. He had

dropped his bag of dirty clothes into his suitcase and was mashing it down to make it fit.

"Mmph," Cole said. It wasn't that he disapproved, exactly. It was just that Gordo might not understand what a pointless exercise dating was. If you found an omni you liked, what could you do with it? You couldn't keep it for long. If you fed from it much it would get addicted. If it didn't get addicted, it got jealous. Even if you didn't feed from it at all, you could only keep it a few years, at best, before it started noticing that you didn't age or—if it had any spirit—carping at the restrictions of your night life. Cruel, anyway, to take it from its friends and family, which is what you had to do if you wanted to spend any reasonable amount of personal time with it.

"Sounds like he's going to have fun," Gordo said as he zipped up his suitcase.

"That's beside the point. *You* are not to have a date. Sandor knows how to read omnis, to play them and release them none the wiser. You do not. Dates are for people who wear self-control and restraint like a second skin—"

"Take it easy. I don't *want* to go on a date."

He said it so positively that Cole was taken a little aback. "Oh," he said. "Good."

"Are we ready?"

"Yes." Now Cole was wondering why Gordo wouldn't want to go on a date. Wasn't that what omnis did? Omnis, and Sandor?

He thought about it some more as he and Gordo left the hotel. Gordo already seemed older than he had back in New York. Cole saw him silently observing their surroundings—taking in the wide street, the columned and bricked campus buildings, the muted colors of the passing cars. The only omni-like moment came when a group of girls paused on the opposite sidewalk.

It would not have occurred to Cole to enjoy their appearance, but when he noticed Gordo's eyes lingering appreciatively over them, he took a second look. And now that he thought about it, that one with the blonde hair did have a rather attractive line from neck to shoulder, from shoulder to waist—fragile bone structure but generous breasts.

As they walked on, leaving the girls behind, Cole had the sudden feeling that he was skimming the surface of his own life.

It was silly; what was he supposed to do about seeing omnis on a public street anyway?

Nothing, that's what.

"Hey, Cole," Gordo said, turning to look over his shoulder after a girl in fishnet stockings, "you know the street dance last night?"

The headlights of the stopped cars were uncomfortably bright, and you couldn't see who was behind the wheel of any of the cars.

"Yes," Cole said. He was trying to recall exactly what Johnny had said, back in four-and-a-half.

It's our ability to feel that keeps us human.

"I saw this Goth guy there with a thing on his finger," Gordo was saying. "Like a tool thing, you know, pointy. It looked a lot easier than these rings. I don't guess there's any way we could use something like that?"

Cole immediately thought of Royal. "What did he look like?"

"You know, Goth. Just . . . *Goth.* Black all over. And the pointy thing."

"Finger guard," Cole corrected. They weren't terribly unusual, among certain types of omnis. "No, we can't use them. They draw attention."

"Yeah, I figured." Gordo sighed.

"The guy—what color was his hair? Was it black too?"

"I dunno. I was mostly just noticing the pointy thing. Why?"

"Did you talk to him?" Cole asked. "What was he doing?"

"I don't know. He was just in the crowd, that's all."

It was highly unlikely that Gordo had seen Royal. They were almost four hundred miles from Phildelphia. Why would the stray have followed them so far when he'd run away from them back in Philly?

Still, to be safe, Cole would mention it to Sandor, so they could keep an eye out. Just in case.

They fed at the college library. Cole was pleased to see Gordo prowling the stacks like any other student desperately trying to finish a paper on a Sunday night.

He wasn't so pleased when they were back at the hotel and Gordo took Sandor at his word, asking to see Cole's photos.

Cole couldn't think of any reason to refuse—it wasn't as if the photos were private, or secret, or would reveal

243

anything he wanted to keep hidden. Okay, so he had an uncomfortable inkling that he wasn't quite rational in his feelings about them. More reason to bring them out into the light of day, so to speak.

So he brought the file case over to Gordo's room, and, opening it, took out all the various stacks and spread them on the bed. Gordo looked them over for a moment before picking up one of the batches from the fifties.

He started flipping through.

After a moment, Cole picked up a stack he'd taken among the families who lived in the oil fields of Oklahoma. As he looked at each picture, he felt nothing. He thought maybe that was because Gordo was in the room, but it was also possible, he decided with a bit of discomfort, that he'd let too much time go by since the last time he'd looked. He'd briefly perused that one stack at the hotel in—where was it?—but before that he couldn't recall the last time he'd even opened the case.

Gordo went through the pictures, careful not to touch the surfaces. "It's like the edges are cut off on all of them," he said after a while. "I mean, they're not centered. Like this one, see?"

Cole glanced at the one he held out; it showed a little girl, swinging. Cole could remember taking it; her dress was gray in the picture, but in life it had been cherry red, with a white collar. She was caught in midflight at the height of her swing, at the exact point between rising and falling. Her hair was lofted chaotically into her face, but even the hair couldn't hide the smile of pure joy.

"See her feet?" Gordon said. "And her head, and the top of the swing set, and the house? It's like . . ."

"What?"

"I dunno. Like she goes on beyond the edge of the picture. All of these are like that. Like there's all kinds of stuff going on beyond the edges."

Cole bent closer to see the photo. He did not touch it.

"That's right," he said. "It's her life."

"Her life?"

"It goes on beyond the edges of the picture. This is just one moment, one feeling."

"She looks really happy."

"Happy. Yes."

"But you said you're not taking these anymore."

"No."

"Why not?"

"I don't enjoy it now."

Gordo gave him a long look, but said nothing. He went back to the photos.

Cole put down his stack and sat in the armchair. He watched Gordo finish the stack in his hand, then pick up another. The kid went through them pretty quickly, only occasionally stopping to look more closely, when one caught his eye.

He held up a photo to show Cole. "Who killed him?"

It was the little boy in the white sailor suit. "No one," Cole said. "He died of disease. Why would you think someone killed him?"

"I dunno. I just thought maybe . . . I dunno." He put the picture back into the stack and started leafing through again. "Hey. Cole. Did *you* ever kill anyone?"

It was an unexpected question. Bluntly put, but honestly asked. Cole knew he meant killing in the feed. It was something Gordo would be interested in. And it was something that Cole ought to explain, in order to show Gordo how he had to learn to relate to the rest of the world.

So he answered. "Yes."

"Who?"

"A girl."

"What happened?"

All right. This was part of his responsibility. He was here to let Gordo know all aspects of a heme's position. He, Cole, had a concrete example to share. If he had to rake over a couple of raw nerves to do it, that was a small price to pay to prevent Gordo from making the same mistake. And Gordo would remember the lesson better if it had real people attached to it.

Cole had never spoken baldly of what he'd done, never told it out loud as one entire experience. He could do it though. Enough time had passed that he ought to be able to speak of it without emotion. The same way he had told Gordo about his first feed.

It took him a moment to compose himself though. He did not look forward to seeing that horrified, fascinated, omni-ish look on Gordo's face. Not about this.

Gordo was still looking through the pictures in his hand—photos of strangers. How much easier it was to talk about strangers!

"Okay," Cole said, committing himself. "Gordo. Do you remember when I told you what happens to us in sun?"

"Yeah."

"The reason I know what it's like is that I . . . made an error once. Oh, put those damn pictures down and sit."

247

Gordo perched on the edge of the bed. He held the stack of photos for another moment, then laid it carefully on the bed and turned his attention to Cole.

"When I was like you," Cole began. "Actually, a bit older . . . but anyway. I was . . . fearful. Alone. I don't know—probably you haven't felt this yet, but you get to a point where you see that every living thing is passing you by."

"Like spring," Gordo reminded him. "Like you said in the kitchen that time."

"Yes. It can start with a feeling of disconnection. Do you understand what I mean?"

"A little bit. Ever since this thing happened to me, it's like I can't keep my feet on the ground, like I can't be sure what's real anymore. Out here with you guys, it feels like things are more solid. But back at the Building I could just not think and not face anything. It was like I was floating."

"Yes, that's part of it. But later, you may get a feeling of being passed by and left alone. . . ." He wasn't explaining this well enough. He had to do better, make the kid aware of what might come. Had to make him *understand.*

"All right. Now. Don't talk, just listen. I saw it like this: All of life on Earth was like a river. Everyone on Earth was floating down this river, and I had to stand alone on the bank, watching them all go by. I got to a point where I realized that every single person around me would always be out of my grasp, always disappearing around the bend to a fate that I could never see. Does that make any sense to you?"

Gordo nodded. Cole drew a deep breath and continued.

"I still thought I could get attached to omnis. I thought I halfway still *was* one, I suppose." He felt a sudden, irrational desire to babble that he had never meant any harm—but he ignored it and pressed grimly on. "And there was this girl, a young lady, who did not know what I was. But I was stupid. I thought that— that—" What was wrong with him? He did not usually have trouble verbalizing whatever was in his head. "I thought that I could *feel* my way through a situation and everything would turn out all right. I think I had faith in God, or the universe, or something—faith that if you have good intentions, things will eventually work out for the best.

"Anyway, what happened was that I—stupidly—

thought I could create a companion for myself. I let myself think that she was my . . . soul mate, I suppose, although there wasn't really a word for it back then. And I, being stupid—I can't stress that enough, Gordo— let myself get attached. I let myself think that it was meant to be."

He had felt his face getting hot for some time, and it dawned on him: That must mean it was turning red. "I'm uncomfortable telling you all this," he admitted. He *had* to be honest. It was his own actions, after all, that had resulted in shame and embarrassment. "But I wouldn't be doing my duty if I didn't allow you to learn from my mistakes.

"So one romantic summer night I did it. I killed her, with love, with what I thought were good intentions."

"On purpose?" Gordo didn't seem to be shocked. He sounded as if he were just making sure.

"Yes," Cole said. "And it never occurred to me that I hadn't even *asked* her. I'd never told her what I was. I never stopped to think that half of her affection for me was the usual omni-heme attraction and that the other half was the mysterious life's tragedy I kept hinting at. Anyway. There's a lot more to it, but suffice it to say

250

that she hated me. And she was completely justified in doing so. It was quite a jolt for me to be jerked around to her point of view. To see that my good intentions were really selfish and small-minded.

"But we were stuck together for a while. I had to live side by side with the one person I wanted and couldn't have, and she was trapped with the one person she despised most in the entire universe. It was torture. She left me for other hemes as soon as she was able, and I ended up traveling with Sandor and Frederick for a while. I saw her occasionally, because she'd check in with Johnny—he was in the process of creating the Colony—but she was very cold to me. Wouldn't speak to or look at me if she could avoid it at all.

"And then Johnny bought the Building. It was always his dream, to provide a safe place for all of us. You don't know Johnny very well, but I can tell you that if it wasn't for him, most of us American hemes would be underground, in the dark.

"Anyway, Bess—Elizabeth—she came when we had only been moved in for a few years. She was different that time. Still avoiding me, but not so spiteful. She seemed sad, and tired. I didn't try to talk to her about it. I was

251

afraid to force the issue. But I *should* have tried. Because early one afternoon she threw herself off the roof.

"You can imagine, if you fall five or six stories, what it does to you. I don't know how long she lay there in the sun. No one could help her. She was dead, the omnis thought—and no wonder; she was pretty well smashed up. And by the time Johnny got her back, her bones had knit themselves back together—but they hadn't been set, you see, so they were a bit . . . misshapen. Her internal organs had healed. Her skin had begun to renew itself. The only thing that hadn't healed in any way was her mind. And that wasn't from the fall but from the sun."

And that was it, he thought. He'd done rather well—gotten out the pertinent facts, not glossed over his own errors.

"How did Johnny get her back?" Gordo asked.

"Bribed. Lied. Stole."

"Oh. I thought maybe he ran out real quick and carried her in."

"God, no. *Nobody* could do that. I'm the only one who was stupid enough to try."

He hadn't intended to mention that part. It had been horrible—his outer layers of skin falling in white lacy shreds, the flesh underneath red raw meat. Every nerve exposed. He'd had to turn back after only a few seconds of direct sunlight.

It took him a moment to realize that Gordo had asked him a question. "Sorry, what?" he said.

"She didn't die, right?"

"Of course not."

"So where is she now?"

"She's in the Building," Cole said. "Up on the fifth floor." He noticed suddenly that he wasn't looking at Gordo—that he hadn't been able to for some time. So now he forced himself to lift his head, ready to see the kid gawking at him.

But Gordo's face showed nothing of the kind. No shock, no horror.

Cole could not *tell* what Gordo was thinking. It was a little disconcerting, as if he'd lost his footing unexpectedly while Gordo was standing steady.

That was a silly thought. He'd gotten the information out. Said what needed to be said—*more* than what needed to be said. Now they were done with the subject. Lesson taught. Over. Finished.

He reached for a stack. "Are we through looking at

these?" he asked Gordo.

"I am. So is she up there all by herself?"

Methodically Cole began to put each stack in its proper place in the file case. "No, she's never left alone. The others take turns watching over her." He frowned down at the photos in his hand—couldn't remember which ones they were, which section of the case they belonged in. "And Johnny checks in on her every day." The top picture was of women running a race during a town picnic. Their dresses flared back above their ankles, showing black stockings and button shoes; their hair was piled up high; their arms were caught midpump.

"Do you go visit her?" Gordo asked.

Cole stuffed the stack into an empty slot. "There's no point." He wasn't going to try to explain what it felt like to look into the eyes of someone you loved and see an inhuman something looking out at you. Wasn't going to describe what it's like when the mind of the person you care about has been evicted from her body. And to know that you had caused it. "No point," he repeated, more firmly. "She doesn't recognize anyone. Doesn't remember anything that happened, whether it was a hundred years or merely a hundred seconds ago. Seeing me—

seeing *anyone*—does nothing for her; and—and—there's just no point."

He picked up another stack and shoved it into the file.

"I'm sorry," he heard Gordo say, with such sincere sympathy that it gave Cole that odd, disoriented feeling again.

"Sounds kind of like what I did with Jill," Gordo added.

"No, it's completely different." Last stack. Cole shut the flap and snapped the elastic around it, suddenly weary.

But it didn't matter how weary he was. He was here to explain things, no matter whether he was tired, or hurting—no matter what he felt; he had a responsibility to fulfill. "Thirst," he told Gordo, keeping his voice even, "is a physical need. Our bodies *need* blood the way they *need* oxygen. You may deny the need to breathe, but your lungs will eventually force you to breathe anyway. What you did was out of your control. What *I* did was completely unnecessary."

He got up and took the file over to his suitcase. He hoped the kid would let it go now.

"Yeah, but you loved her," Gordo pointed out. "You didn't mean to hurt her."

Cole could feel himself starting to get angry—why,

he wasn't quite sure; but he knew it wasn't the least bit helpful, so he said nothing and tried to push it down.

"You didn't mean for it to work out the way it did," Gordo went on.

Cole put the file folder back in the pocket of the suitcase. "Let's just drop it."

"So, really," Gordo continued, "we *are* basically in the same boat."

"I said, let's drop it."

"Okay, but the point is, I know how you feel, dude."

Enough. Cole zipped his suitcase with one quick gesture. Then he turned to Gordo. "You know nothing," he said, low and deadly even. "A few weeks ago you were . . . eating cooked animal flesh and downing six-packs. You know *less* than nothing."

He hadn't raised his voice at all. Hadn't made one move toward Gordo. Yet Gordo sat stunned. He looked as if Cole had struck him.

For just a moment—then his mouth tightened. "Is that why you act like you're better than me all the time?"

"I don't do that."

"Yes, you do. You talk to me like I'm an idiot. 'Tighten

256

the cap on your shampoo,'" Gordo mimicked. "'Get rid of the red shirt.'"

"That's not—"

"'*You* are not to have sexual contact. *You* are not to have a date. *You* are not to do anything at all because you're a fucking *idiot*, Gordo.'"

"Just because—"

"Leave me alone." Gordo picked up the remote and switched on the TV.

Okay.

It was fine with Cole if they didn't talk. Cole didn't need anybody explaining his own past to him. So he'd hurt the kid's feelings. So what? He wasn't here to make friends. Besides, teenage guys said worse to each other every day.

Cole wanted to go back to his own room. *Really* leave the kid alone. But he knew he couldn't. It was his responsibility—his burden—to stick with Gordo, no matter what.

They sat together in stiff silence for the rest of the night.

CHAPTER EIGHTEEN

BY the next evening Cole regretted snapping at the kid. *Eating cooked animal flesh and downing six-packs*—for God's sake, he had quoted *Frederick* at the boy!

And Gordo had obviously taken it to heart. As they left the hotel, Cole could see that he was still out of sorts. He didn't wait to hand his suitcase to Cole, who stood in front of the open trunk, but tossed the bag in himself before walking around to get in.

Cole gave Sandor a questioning glance.

Sandor just shrugged.

When they were on the road again, Cole studied Gordo in the mirror. The kid was in his usual place in the backseat. But he slouched into the corner as if he'd collapsed there, and dark circles under his eyes gave his face a weary look.

Cole remembered now what Gordo had told him: *Ever since this thing happened to me, it's like I can't keep my feet on the ground. Out here with you guys, it feels like things are more solid.*

"Gordo," he said, "I'm sorry I snapped at you last night."

Gordo didn't say it was all right. Lights from oncoming cars seemed to slide over his shoulders and face before dropping into shadows.

Cole thought he wasn't going to speak at all, but after a few moments, he asked stiffly, "Where are we going?"

"I don't know," Cole answered.

"Don't you have some kind of *plan*?" He sounded like the same sulky, sullen kid Cole had met that first night in the Building.

"It doesn't matter much where we go right now. We can work on basics anywhere."

"Anywhere?" Gordo sat up. "Then why don't we go to Missouri?"

"Missouri is not an option," Cole reminded him. He did not explain. He knew why Gordo wanted to go there. And Gordo knew why they couldn't.

259

Gordo slumped back in his seat again. When he spoke this time, his voice was laced with bitterness.

"I'm sick of you guys."

Concerned, Sandor started to turn around.

"Let him be," Cole advised.

Sandor sighed and turned back.

"How's that look?" Cole nodded at a sign ahead on the right. It stood in front of a large building with lots of cars parked around it and a sign announcing that Thursday was Ladies' Nite.

"Very nice," Sandor said, a little too heartily.

Once inside, Cole was relieved to see that Gordo's mood didn't affect his hunting. The basics *were* becoming second nature to the boy. His feed was effortless, quick, and unnoticed. He chose a slow song for a slow dance. He had the moves to the neck down pat. He didn't walk away the moment he was done but stayed to finish the dance, talking to his feed as an omni would so as not to attract attention.

"He's coming along," Cole admitted to Sandor as they sat at a small table crammed up against a pillar.

"He's homesick," Sandor told Cole. "I heard him crying during the day."

"Crying?" No wonder the kid looked tired.

"Yes. It seems to have hit him all of a sudden: *Boom!* Like a tidal wave."

Gordon's had his whole life ripped away from him, Johnny had said. *You and Sandor are the only way he has of making sense of it all.*

Gordo needed someone to be steady. That someone was Cole—and Cole had dropped the ball.

Okay. He couldn't go back and fix it. He felt bad for the kid, bad for losing his temper last night—but he mustn't let pity or guilt keep him from continuing to teach the boy survival skills. That's what he'd done with Bess. And the more he'd backed off, the worse things had gotten.

"The thing to do," Cole told Sandor, "is not get sucked into his drama. We have to stay focused, no matter what his mood is. We have to be . . . solid."

"Like rocks along the shore." Sandor stirred his straw around in his drink. "So that Gordo has something to cling to when the waves break over him."

"Well . . . yes. I guess."

"It's a good analogy, especially for a heme, don't you think? I should have been a writer." Sandor dropped the

261

straw back into the untouched glass. "Now I'm going to go feed, if you don't mind. I see a little redhead over there. I've always been partial to redheads, and I feel that I could use some cheering up."

"Go ahead," said Cole. "I'll be the rock along the shore until Gordo comes back."

They were all finished shortly after and able to move on quite soon—a huge improvement over the first few nights when Gordo had taken hours to get sustenance.

They had been traveling vaguely southwest, but Cole thought it might be better now to head east again—the opposite direction from Missouri.

And after they got back in the car, he *knew* it was better.

"Since *I'm* the only one who wants to go anywhere," Gordo announced the second the doors were shut, "*I* say we go to Missouri."

Cole cast a glance at him in the rearview mirror but said nothing.

"I want to check on Jill."

Cole felt Sandor looking at him. He shook his head slightly to remind Sandor: *Don't get sucked into the drama.*

"I want . . . I want to see my *mom*." Gordo's voice cracked slightly on the last word.

Sandor turned around, full of sympathy. "Oh, Gordo—"

"No," Cole interrupted. "You have to cut them loose. One more time, Gordo: They are aging and will die. You won't."

"I—I already talked to my mother," Gordo said in a rush. "I called her earlier while Sandor was in the shower."

"Oh, my God," Cole said in disgust. "Did you tell her where you were?"

"No."

"You called her from the room?" Sandor echoed. "What did you say to her, Gordo?"

"I told her I was better now and that I missed her."

Cole fought his urge to snap at the kid again. The last Gordo's mother had heard, he'd turned into Jack the Ripper and run off into the dark. And the kid called her out of the blue to say he was *better now*?

God, hadn't the kid heard anything Cole said?

"How did she take it?" Sandor was asking Gordo.

Gordo shrugged and looked away.

"I'll tell you how she took it," Cole said dryly. "*Not well.*"

"I knew she'd be worried about me." Gordo's voice was muffled.

"Do you think she's less worried now?"

Gordo did not answer. He leaned his forehead against the window.

"We'll talk about it sometime in the future," Sandor said. "Maybe you could see them after a few years, when you are more self-sufficient."

"When I'm no longer responsible for you," Cole said. "I'm telling you right now; we are not going to Missouri on my watch." He waited another moment, willing himself to remain calm and steady—like Sandor said, a rock along the shore. "All right," he said, more to himself than to anyone. "Let's get back to business."

He started the car, but when he turned to make sure the way was clear to back up, he noticed something.

"You're not buckled," he told Gordo, trying beyond all patience to keep his voice even. He pulled out of the parking space, expecting the boy to sullenly buckle up and then sit there in his gloomy corner for the rest of the night.

Cole was heading toward the exit before he realized

that the kid hadn't moved.

He hit the brakes. "Gordo. Buckle your seat belt."

"What difference does it make?" Gordo said coldly. "You said I can't die."

"Nobody said anything about dying. I just don't want to get a ticket."

"Gordo, please," said Sandor.

Cole pulled up the emergency brake and put the car in park. He watched in the mirror, waiting.

And waiting.

After an uncomfortable couple of minutes and a honk from a car that couldn't get by, Gordo finally gave in and fastened the seat belt.

With bad grace, Cole noticed. It was irritating, but Cole said nothing, just pulled onto the highway.

"At least I *want* to check on Jill." Gordo's voice came from the backseat. "At least *I* didn't just walk off and leave her locked up somewhere."

Silence came down like a cold curtain over the car.

Cole's fingers curled tight around the steering wheel. *I didn't* leave *her*, he wanted to say. *She's well cared for.*

No. No. He must disengage himself. This wasn't about him. It was about Gordo. Gordo was firing off arrows because he was angry and upset.

In the backseat, Gordo sank into his corner again.

How predictable.

Cole should never have told the kid all that stuff about Bess. At least he shouldn't have gone into detail the way he had. What had he been thinking? He'd treated the kid—okay, fine, *almost* as if he were a friend. At least for a short time he had. For a few minutes there. And the kid had stuck a knife in his back.

Gordo just leaned against the window, looking out.

To Cole, it felt as if the boy wore his feelings all over his body. Being around him made Cole feel saturated, almost sticky, with residue from his gloom.

CHAPTER NINETEEN

COLE made sure the next motel they stopped at had a pool. He couldn't wait to get away from the rotten little punk. Let Sandor stay in the room with him; Sandor could dole out support and understanding. Whatever else was wrong, the kid sure hadn't been lacking for someone to pat him on the back and be his buddy.

Cole waited in front of his own door, watching to make sure Gordo and Sandor got into their room. As soon as their door shut, he stuck his key card into the slot.

But as he turned the handle, Sandor was back, standing at his shoulder. "Are you all right?" he whispered.

Cole opened the door and set down his suitcase. "I'm fine," he said, but he was annoyed to feel his face getting

267

warm for the second time in two nights. He stepped in and flipped on the lights.

Sandor stayed in the doorway. "I'm surprised you told him about all that. You're usually as closemouthed as a clam."

"I'm regretting it now, let me tell you."

"Oh, don't regret it. You can't control how people respond to your overtures. It was good of you to reach out in the first place."

"Is that what it was?" Cole said. "Reaching out?"

"Yes, and don't let this discourage you."

"I'm not discouraged. I'm just taking it as it comes. Now if you don't mind babysitting the Missouri Kid, I'm going to go for a swim."

This hotel pool was a small rectangle, rigidly outlined in concrete. Good enough.

Cole swam laps—back and forth, back and forth—until his frustration had worked itself loose and was beaten aside by the sheer repetition and effort of exercise.

His arms had begun to feel rubbery, so he turned over and floated on his back for a while, staring up at the sky. He listened to his lungs draw in each long, slow breath and then release it even more slowly.

When he got out, the night air was a little cool on his wet skin, so he wrapped the towel around his shoulders before stretching out in one of the white lounges.

The moon was out, bright white, clouds sliding quickly across it to be outlined briefly in silver before moving on. He'd managed to put his irritation aside, but he couldn't help thinking about what Sandor had said.

Cole hadn't been reaching out. No, it had just been a lesson for Gordo, that's all. And the kid *was* an idiot. He thought good intentions made up for a bad outcome. He was wrong.

Cole knew. He had sat there with Bess curled up against him, his arm curved around her, and he'd thought it out. Decided that Fate had offered a lifeline. There, beside him, was the chance to have a companion—not just any companion, but the companion of his heart.

So he'd taken her life from her—fused her body to her eternal soul so that the soul could never, ever escape. He hadn't thought about that at the time. He'd thought only of himself, of what *he* wanted. What *he* was missing.

It didn't matter if no one else blamed him. It didn't matter if everyone else had moved on. The one person who could absolve him was gone, disappeared into her own shell of a body.

He let himself think about that shell. It was a particular torture he only used on rare occasions, but he brought it out now: bones healed askew. Head permanently at an awkward angle on her once-broken neck. Horrible.

It *was* horrible. The worst thing he'd ever seen.

So . . . why didn't the picture bring its usual stab of self-loathing?

He was tired. That's what it was. The swimming had worn him out. And maybe the events of this trip had burdened him to capacity, so that there were no available feelings left to be whipped to shreds.

Still, it was a little strange. And hard to explain. How could the worst thing he'd ever experienced be . . . just another picture in his head?

CHAPTER TWENTY

COLE stayed in his own room the rest of that night, avoiding Gordo completely. The next evening, not knowing what to expect, he arranged his features into a neutral expression and wheeled his suitcase toward Sandor and Gordo's room.

Funny—only a couple of weeks ago he'd longed for silence, but now the thought of spending a whole night in a quiet and tense car was unappealing.

When Sandor let him in, the blow-dryer was going in the bathroom. Cole thought that was a good sign; maybe Gordo had gotten the bile out of his system.

Sandor took his place on the bed, leaning against the headboard, and Cole seated himself in the scrubby tweed armchair, preparing to be inundated by the TV news Sandor had been watching.

But the TV shut off with a click. The picture shrank instantly into nothingness, leaving the screen a blank.

Cole looked around to see Sandor holding the remote. "Gordo is very unhappy," he informed Cole.

"Ah." Maybe not quite out of his system yet.

"I have come up with an idea to help him," Sandor said. "We should get him a dog."

"That's not funny."

"I'm completely serious. We could go by a pet store. What do you think?" He sat looking at Cole, eager and hopeful.

He *was* serious.

"You're *insane*," Cole burst out. "I can't even believe you'd say something like that."

"They have very small dogs these days, and little bags to carry them in. We could get a quiet one, who only wants to sit with his master and be held. Wouldn't it be nice to be able to provide a helpless creature with everything in the world it desired? And look at it this way. If Gordo gets into a difficulty, he can feed off the dog!"

"That's disgusting."

"Come now. You know that you yourself have been in a pinch once in a while—"

"That's not the same thing as carrying a dog around for a snack. God, it reeks of—of—of the way Frederick treats his omnis!"

"Except that Gordo will love his dog, as Frederick does not love his omnis. I see it now: The boy has lost one life and doesn't feel connected to the new one yet. A dog would help him through the transition."

"A *dog* is not going to help."

"I disagree."

"Sandor, nobody has a dog. Nobody! Where do you think Gordo's going to keep it? In the car? In hotel rooms? Is he going to take it with him every time he feeds?"

"Actually," Sandor said, "I think it might help him get a little closer to the girls. Girls love little dogs, you know. He could tuck a Chihuahua or a Yorkie under his jacket. Or even a mutt—you can tell how big a puppy will get by the size of its paws, you know. If we got one with paws about the size of Q-tips—"

"No. *No!*"

"But we must do *something* for him. I have been trying to remember what it was like when I was new to all this. Things were much simpler then, back in Boravia

273

when I was a boy. But even so I was wild, cruel, self-absorbed for many long years. It's the same with all of us. Including *you*," Sandor said pointedly. "There's no denying that one commits thoughtless acts when one is young, lonely, and afraid. One commits acts that cannot be taken back; is it not so? Do you know what I am saying, Cole?"

Cole shook his head. He didn't trust himself to speak.

"A dog would help him feel more connected."

"Sandor. It's a logistical impossibility."

"It would give him something to feel. If we want to remain human beings, we must feel; don't you agree?"

The blow-dryer stopped.

"All right," said Sandor. "We will set the discussion aside for now."

"We're going to set it aside *forever*. There's no way, Sandor. Do you understand? No way in hell."

He was so vehement about the whole thing that he had trouble clearing the emotion from his face when the bathroom door clicked open and Gordo came out.

Cole gave Sandor one warning look—*Don't you dare say anything about a dog!*—then turned, ready to give Gordo a calm, removed, no-hard-feelings nod of greeting.

But Gordo would not look at him. The kid brought his things out in a big pile, deliberately dumped them into his open suitcase with his old sloppiness, and zipped up the suitcase without a word.

Cole decided *he* would not speak either. Even if he wanted to, what could he say: *The sooner you drop the attitude, the sooner everything will get back to normal*?

Gordo's "normal" was long gone.

All three were silent in the car. Cole hoped Sandor wasn't thinking about dogs.

Cole quickly spotted a likely place for a feed, a box-like bar. He disliked bars and had hoped to gradually get away from them; the omnis in them had often had too much to drink and were smelly breathed and repetitive. But bars were still easiest for Gordo, and Gordo wasn't at his most agreeable right now, so that was where they must go.

Cole had already passed the exit, so he had to double back. Another glance in the mirror, and he had to fight the urge to inform Gordo that he looked like a duck when he was pouting.

"All right," he said when they were in the parking lot, "I guess we're ready."

He turned off the engine and got out of the car, feeling to make sure his wallet was in his back pocket as he walked around to Sandor's side.

Gordo had not emerged.

Cole peered in: The kid was still buckled and showed no signs of moving. So Cole gave the window a sharp rap.

Slowly, deliberately, Gordo turned his head to give Cole a seething blast of a dirty look.

All right, so he was still upset. Cole made a rolling-down-the-window gesture at Gordo; he would talk to him, lay out the choices calmly.

But Gordo ignored him.

Sandor had gotten out, and the front passenger door was still open. Cole bent into the car to look back at Gordo.

"Is there a problem?" he asked. If his voice had a slightly acid tone to it, he still felt he was being reasonably polite, under the circumstances.

"I'm not going to do it."

"Not going to do what?" Cole glanced back at the box-like building. He didn't like bars either, and it wasn't the nicest place in the world; but it wasn't a dive either. Gordo, he felt, was in no position to object.

"Any of it. I'm not going to drink people's blood any-more. The whole thing's sick. I'd rather starve."

In a rush, Cole felt as if he were standing outside himself, watching from a distance. He was standing in a potholed parking lot in god-knew-which city, trying to talk sense to a hemovore who thought he had an aversion to drinking blood.

Sandor leaned in now. "Gordo. I know it's hard, but you must get out of the car."

"No," said Gordo, stubborn.

"It's not sick at all," Sandor wheedled. "It's perfectly clean. Perfectly humane. More so than the cows killed to make the hamburgers you ate a few weeks ago."

"I didn't eat any hamburgers a few weeks ago. I haven't had a hamburger in months."

Sandor put his whole upper body into the car. "I'm sorry for everything that's happened to you," Cole heard him say, dripping with sympathy. "I know it's a difficult adjustment. But you need to feed."

"I'm never feeding again." Gordo sounded as if he meant it.

This time Sandor emerged to shake his head sadly at Cole.

Okay. Cole grabbed the handle of Gordo's door and pulled it open. This kid was worse than an omni. At least omnis either followed directions or were easily manipulated.

"You will feed," Cole informed Gordo. "And you're going to do it now."

Gordo's eyes narrowed. "No. I'm not. So back off."

Sandor looked at Cole and shrugged: *What should we do?*

What indeed? They couldn't physically force the kid to feed. If there was some kind of reverse psychology or cajoling that would work, Cole didn't know what it was.

He slammed Gordo's door shut and stood for a moment, trying to think.

"We'll move on," he decided. "Gordo's trying to manipulate us into going to Missouri. Which we are *not*. So if he doesn't want to feed, fine. He's not used to missing a meal. At least, he hasn't missed any since I've known him."

"Definitely not used to it," Sandor agreed. "In the Building, every time I came around a corner, there he was, feeding off someone."

"Charming. Let's just get in the car and go. Likely

278

he'll be ready when we stop for the day."

At least, he thought as he got into the car, *the kid's seat belt is buckled.*

They did try again, as they hit the outskirts of Wheeling. Sandor and Cole both saw the billboard at almost the same time and exchanged glances.

"Gordo," Sandor said, "look at that billboard."

It was an advertisement for a gentlemen's club, a girl curled seductively on her side.

Cole thought he'd better let Sandor do the talking. Sandor was better at this sort of thing than he was.

"I'll bet you're curious to see inside a place like that, aren't you, Gordo?" Sandor asked.

Cole could see that Gordo *was* curious; he didn't move his head, but Cole could see his eyes following the billboard as they passed.

"Two more exits," Sandor said. "Let's try it. Gordo, I'm sure you will find some lovely—"

"You two can go. I'm not leaving this car."

Cole had a sinking feeling that the project was doomed, but he pulled off the freeway at the proper exit and found the place without difficulty. It seemed to be in a building that had once been something else, such as a theme restaurant or a miniature golf place, with wooden planks for walls and a square tower rising in the middle.

Again Gordon refused to get out. Just sat there like a lump with Cole and Sandor waiting outside the open car door.

"Exactly what do you hope to accomplish by all this?" Cole asked.

"I hope to die," Gordon said. "That's what I'm going to do: I'm going to die. Or hibernate, or whatever you call it. I'd rather starve than live like this anymore."

"Don't be melodramatic," Cole said, exasperated. "You won't starve. You'll lose control first."

"Watch me."

"It's not about *watching* you. You can try all you want, but you'll fail. And the longer you wait, the more spectacularly you'll fail."

"You don't know me. When I want something bad enough, I go for it. I've held my breath till I passed out."

His arms were crossed; his face was like stone.

He meant every word he said. The kid really *meant* it.

Cole shut Gordo's door and walked around to the driver's side.

"Now what?" Sandor said over the roof of the car. "Do

you want to move on, or should you and I go ahead and feed, or what?"

Cole bent to give Gordo a quick glance. Even in the shadows of the backseat, he radiated anger.

"We can't force him to go in," Cole told Sandor. "And he shouldn't be left alone. You go ahead, and I'll stay out here."

"Are you sure?"

"Yes. I need to think anyway."

Sandor disappeared inside, and Cole got into the car again. Gordo was a lump in the back.

Cole ignored him.

If Gordon gets completely out of hand, Johnny had said. *If you feel he's becoming a danger to the rest of us.*

Gordo *wasn't* getting out of hand—no, the kid was just having a little tantrum, that was all. He didn't have the focus to hold off feeding for very long. He'd probably forget about his little rebellion by tomorrow night.

But if he didn't? If he continued to refuse?

Cole leaned his head back against the headrest. He knew his body appeared relaxed, calm, but he felt as if the kid were edging him up against a cliff, forcing him to fight to keep his footing.

Gordo still sat in his usual spot. He hadn't said a

word. But after a few moments a soft noise began to intrude on the silence in the car, at intervals, so low that at first Cole thought it was the wind, or something far down the street.

But when he finally lifted his head and looked around, he saw that it was Gordo.

The kid had fallen asleep. He was still tightly buckled, sitting upright against the seat back, but his eyes were closed and his head drooped to one side. His mouth had relaxed and from this came the deep, regular sound of breathing.

He looked as if he couldn't hurt a fly.

Cole turned around again. He sat staring at the car parked ahead of him, considering.

Likely the boy was simply worn out. Yes, that was it—tired, and overwhelmed.

As soon as Sandor came back, they'd find a place close by. Let the kid have extra downtime. Maybe he just needed a night off from feeding. Maybe a good day's sleep would solve the problem.

Maybe tomorrow night he'd wake up agreeable and willing again, and with his feet back on the ground.

CHAPTER TWENTY-ONE

SLEEP did *not* help Gordo.

The next evening started off as a repeat of the one previous. Cole was sitting on the edge of the bed, waiting, when Gordo came out of the bathroom. He flung his belongings into his suitcase, then himself into a chair, where he sat, glaring at nothing.

His death wish didn't extend to letting his hair go uncoiffed, Cole noted with some acerbity.

Sandor went into the bathroom to make sure they weren't leaving anything behind. "I guess that's it," he said to Cole as he came out. Then he added a little louder, "Gordo, are you ready?"

Gordo ignored him.

"What kind of place would you like to try tonight?" Sandor continued, as if nothing was wrong, as if the kid wasn't sulking like a two-year-old omni. "Would you like to learn about feeding in movie theaters?"

Gordo didn't even look around. "*You* go wherever you want. *I'm* not feeding."

There was no question now. The kid had drawn an invisible circle around himself. All matters heme were now shut out.

Or so he thought. But Cole knew better.

Gordo might *look* as if he wouldn't hurt a fly, but he would—and much, much worse.

Cole thought about it as he pulled out of the hotel parking lot. God—what if Gordo didn't feed, and didn't feed, and finally went wild? What if he lost control in a hotel, in public; what if he attacked someone who was walking by? What if he jumped out of the car while it was moving?

Johnny had said it wouldn't come to that—but clearly Johnny was wrong. The boy *wasn't* doing fine.

And it was Cole's responsibility to see that Gordo *didn't* get out of control. That's what he'd signed up for.

He eased up the freeway ramp, driving as carefully as ever. But his stomach twisted into a sour knot at the thought of what he might have to do to solve this problem. He couldn't help but wonder what had gone through the mind of that Old World heme when the predawn light had begun to glow between the boards of that shed.

Morning light was mechanical, inhuman. Once it started rolling over the horizon it was relentless. What had that heme felt as it came?

What would Gordo feel?

God. The kid didn't deserve to be tortured into a brittle shell of a human being just because he was an omni-ish dope.

Cole noticed that he was gripping the steering wheel too hard. He relaxed his fingers, flexing them. He could not afford to get emotional or panicked about this. He had to push emotion aside and *think*.

The bottom line was that missing an occasional night of feeding wasn't a big deal. Two nights of refusal wouldn't hurt anybody either.

Before the third night was out, though, the kid would probably start to feel it. As the evening wore on, Thirst would start to uncurl in his body. He'd likely give in pretty quickly then, not being used to feeling any Thirst at all.

But if he didn't?

By the fourth night Gordo's instinct to feed would be stronger than any internal promise, any stubbornness. Cole himself had managed to go longer than that a few times, long ago.

They were now on night number two.

Okay. Cole still had tonight and at least part of tomorrow night before anything happened. He could get this turned around.

He *would* get this turned around.

Sandor was subdued, looking out the window at the passing businesses and office parks. Gordo leaned against the door; Cole could only see part of his shoulder and head in the mirror.

Methodically, Cole thought through everything he knew about control and Thirst. He knew quite a bit; more than he should have. It wasn't something he liked to remember; he had let it all fall into a general hole somewhere in the back of his brain, because bringing it out was pointless and rather cringe inducing.

The fact was, in the years between the time Bess had left him till the moment of her fall, Cole had come as close to having a death wish as a hemovore could. He'd been a lot more experienced than Gordo by then, but there was no denying that he'd done some pretty stupid things.

He began to sort through those things now, ticking off possible courses of action, considering, rejecting—trying to come up with a plan.

When Cole pulled over at a truck stop, Sandor sat up.

"Do we need gas already?" he asked, looking around. The truck stop was good sized, a gas station with a store and restaurant attached.

"No," Cole said. "It's just a change from bars. Ready to feed, Gordo?" he asked, keeping his tone casual.

"No," said Gordo.

"Then you won't mind waiting for us in the car." He didn't bother to keep the coldness out of his voice. As he got out he gave Sandor a glance: *I want to talk to you.*

Inside, the restaurant had a couple of customers. A cashier watched over the store section, but Cole saw a small arcade area next to the restaurant, and that's where he headed, followed by Sandor.

As he'd hoped, no one else was in the arcade. As if by agreement, he and Sandor walked over to the token machine.

"I think maybe we should call Johnny," Sandor said, as Cole pulled out his wallet—Cole didn't really want to play anything, but he didn't want to be accused of loitering either.

"No," he told Sandor. "Johnny might come out here."

"Do you think that would be bad?"

"Not exactly." Cole took out a dollar bill and stuck it in the slot. "It's just that I don't know where Johnny draws the line." Tokens rained down, but he didn't pick them up; he was searching for words to explain what he was thinking. "The way Gordo is right now," he finally told Sandor, "I don't know how Johnny's going to see him. He might see an asset that needs help to reach its potential—or he might just see a liability." Now Cole bent and scooped up the tokens. "Do you know what I mean?"

"Well . . . yes, I suppose. Hmm, try that game by the window. That way we can keep an eye on Gordo."

So they went over to Zombie Death House. Sandor was right; through the window they could see the car, with Gordo slouched in the backseat.

Cole dropped tokens into the slot and took the plastic gun out of its holster.

"I'm not sure Gordo would listen to Johnny anyway," Sandor continued, leaning against the side of the game. "Johnny isn't physically imposing, you know, and he makes suggestions rather than ordering people around. All the time we were in New York, I don't think Gordo ever caught on that Johnny wasn't just some little guy in the back."

"I think we can take care of Gordo on our own anyway." Cole pressed the button and began to play, halfheartedly shooting zombies as they popped out from their hiding places.

"How?"

"We can't force him to feed. There's no way we can keep him from driving himself to the breaking point. What we *can* do is decide where and how the breaking point happens."

"Are you suggesting that we lock him up somewhere?"

"No, no. Just listen for a sec. I figure he'll start feeling it tomorrow or the next night. Do you agree?"

"Yes, definitely."

"Gordo's not used to controlling himself, *and* he's not used to feeling real Thirst." Cole remembered how

289

the kid had lusted after the drops on that girl's finger-tips in New York. "I think we should find a place tonight and then settle in for as long as it takes. Not just any place—the *right* place. Tomorrow evening we'll bring a feed to the room and wait Gordo out. When he shows signs that he's getting antsy, we'll *make* him crack— but at a place and in a manner of our choosing."

RELOAD, the screen said. Belatedly, Cole aimed off screen and pulled the trigger.

"Make him crack," Sandor repeated. "You mean by tempting him as he's on the point of losing control anyway?"

"Exactly. One little puncture at the right time, a whiff of blood, and he'll drop like an overripe fruit."

"Hmm. So when you say 'the right place,' you mean 'cheap hotel in a red-light district.'"

"Maybe *near* a red-light district. I'd like to be able to get *some* sleep."

"I think it's a good plan, Cole. But what about after-ward? What if he pulls this again? Are we to go on tempting him and making him crack every few nights?"

"If we have to. But I don't think he will. That first feed of his was a nightmare. He's already *felt* it wasn't quite real, and the farther he gets from it, the easier for him to *believe* it wasn't real."

"It is rather a sobering thing, to be out of control in that way."

"We'll be with him this time."

"Yes." Sandor sighed. "I hope I don't have to hit him again. By the way," he added, "you're out of ammo. And there's a health pickup on the right."

"What? Oh." Cole reloaded again and fired at the screen without looking. "So we're agreed?" he asked Sandor.

"Yes. Poor little fellow," Sandor said, with another glance at the car. "We have to remember; he's only eighteen. His hormones must be a raging mosh pit of emotion."

"*I'm* eighteen, and *my* hormones aren't a raging mosh pit."

"Maybe yours got worn out already."

INSERT TOKENS TO CONTINUE flashed on the screen. Cole stuck the gun back in its holder. He was missing more zombies than he shot anyway. "Are we ready to go then?"

"Yes. We need to get moving if we want to find a suitable place tonight. But . . . you didn't feed last night, did

291

you? Would you like to find something here? Although it looks like your options are limited at the moment."

Cole looked around. No one was in sight except the cashier, who now leaned against the register, talking to someone on the phone.

Cole quickly weighed the possibilities: subdue the guy in full view of the store security cameras, hide in the bathroom to wait for one of the restaurant customers, or feed later when they stopped for the day.

The cashier laughed into the phone, and Cole saw that his teeth were stained with nicotine.

"I'll wait," he said. Sandor was right; they needed to get moving. He wanted to get out of West Virginia, head as far east as they could get in a few hours—to DC, maybe Baltimore. After they got checked in, he should have time to get a decent feed.

Night number three—he hoped that would be the key.

CHAPTER TWENTY-TWO

THEY found the "right place" in Baltimore, along a street lined with check-cashing places, pawnshops, and bail bondsmen.

The hotel was a two-story rectangle tucked between a corner thrift shop and an abandoned storefront. Its bricks had been painted white—only recently, from the fresh look of the paint—but dark streaks had begun to run down from the roof, which evidently was made from something that didn't stay put during rain. The sign out front was missing the *T* and the *L*, so it said:

VICKERY MO E

UNDER NEW MANAGEMENT

DAILY AND WEEKLY RATES

It was the "daily and weekly rates" that drew Cole. He didn't want anything that rented rooms by the hour.

"The Vickery Moe," read Sandor, as Cole pulled into the lumpy parking lot. "Oh, I like that."

"What's *this*?" Gordo looked up at the dark streaks in disgust.

"*This* is where we're staying until you feed," Cole told him. He felt quite calm, now that he'd lined up a reasonable plan of action. And if the kid thought the Vickery Moe was punishment for not feeding, that was fine with Cole.

In the hotel office, a tiny elderly man sat on a stool behind the desk, watching a small black-and-white TV. His hair was a white mop, his back bent over on itself like a shepherd's crook. He didn't say a word; but as the three hemes came to the desk, he slid down off his stool and hobbled over. The counter came to the middle of his chest.

"One single, one double," said Cole. "We'll be staying at least four nights." That was one of the unfair things about being heme; you had to pay an extra night every time you stayed somewhere, because you could never leave before checkout time in the morning.

The man eyed them. "Twenty-five for a single, forty

for a double, fifteen-dollar deposit."

"Deposit on what?"

"Sheets and towels."

Cole and Sandor exchanged a glance.

"We'll take the sheets and towels," Cole said, and pulled out his wallet.

The little man counted the money carefully and put it in the register. He gave Cole two keys, then reached under the counter and pulled out a white stack of tidily folded linens. He silently pushed them across the counter. Then he hobbled to his stool and climbed back up.

Cole checked the keys: rooms 211 and 213. "Second floor," he told Sandor.

Sandor sniffed the stack in his arms as they walked to the stairs. "They're clean," he whispered. "Thank God."

Room 211 turned out to be the double. The floor was bare grayish green tile. The beds were neatly covered with tan bedspreads. A small window was half filled by an air-conditioning unit, the top draped with a heavy, plastic-looking curtain.

"We have a TV!" Sandor said. "My God, it must be as old as I am. Look, you have to turn a knob to change the channel!"

"A TV, but no phone," Cole told him; a broken wire dangled from the wall by the bed.

"I have my cell. Pillows and blankets in the closet," added Sandor, checking. "You know what this place reminds me of?"

"The bad old days?" said Cole.

"Yes. This is a reminder to be thankful for our blessings. Look, there's a cupcake wrapper under the bed!"

"This place is a dump," Gordo muttered.

Cole said nothing but checked his watch—still a few hours to sunrise; at least two before the sky started lightening.

He entered 213 alone. No TV here, but there was a heavy rotary phone next to the bed. *If you put two eleven and two thirteen together,* he thought, *you'd have one almost-decent hotel room.*

The floor wasn't tile but dark carpet. The light switch by the door didn't work, but the lamp by the bed did. When he turned it on, Cole could see that the old man—or whoever was responsible for cleaning—*had* vacuumed, at least partially, because the vacuum cleaner had left tracks around the bed. He didn't look *under* the bed though; he didn't want to know what the previous occupants had been eating or doing.

Still, this place gave him an odd feeling, as if he'd been here before. He hadn't, of course—but something about it seemed familiar.

The carpet. It was old, brown, with a matted look.

The place reminded him of Royal's lair.

And now he realized that he'd been so preoccupied with Gordo that he'd forgotten about the stray. He'd driven all the way to Baltimore without paying more than usual attention to the rearview mirror. Of course, he *had* been paying attention on the way from Ohio to West Virginia and hadn't seen anything. But that was no excuse. It was likely Gordo had seen some omni back in Castile rather than the stray, but that was no excuse either.

Cole had already dropped the ball once by losing his temper. He couldn't afford to do any more dropping.

Now he intended to grab a quick feed so he'd be fresh for tomorrow, but there was something he had to attend to first. Experience had taught him that windows in places like this sometimes required extra attention, if one wanted to avoid unpleasant surprises during the day.

The Vickery Moe was no exception. The window was like the one in 211, an air conditioner in the bottom half. But this curtain was missing some hooks so that it drooped in spots. Cole would have to take care, not wait till the last minute to get it covered.

He got his things out and set about the task, and was soon glad he'd started on it. The curtain was an odd rubbery material, and the tape wouldn't stick well. It looked likely to fall off during the day, especially when the air conditioner kicked on. Cole ended up digging in the pocket of his suitcase for the wrinkled black garbage bag he kept for emergencies.

He taped that directly to the wall around the window, securing it carefully along the top of the air conditioner. Finally, satisfied, he collected his keys and his wallet.

He'd go hunting on foot tonight. He wanted to get a better idea of the area right around the hotel. He already knew that the cruising strip was less than half a mile away; it would take moments to get there in his car. But he wanted to get a mental picture of the immediate neighborhood.

Because what if Gordo botched it, and they ended up

with a screamer? Or, say, the timing was off, and the kid took a little too much? They'd have to discreetly remove his passed-out feed from room 211 and deposit it somewhere else.

No, Cole wanted to know where the nearest isolated corner was and where the dark alley behind the hotel led. He wanted to know which businesses and dwellings were close and whether anyone was likely to be in them during the night.

There was no room for slackness, no room for carelessness. Cole had his mind on the particulars now: He intended to be prepared.

CHAPTER TWENTY-THREE

COLE headed down the alley behind the Vickery Moe. The ground under his feet was partly paved, partly dirt—a real mess when it rained, he could tell.

A chain-link fence marked the back of the alley. Behind it were small houses, some with windows boarded up, all silent and dark.

On Cole's left were the rear entrances of the small businesses that lined the street beyond. The first few backed directly up to the alley; but as the fence ended on Cole's right, opening into a vacant lot, the brick wall and doorways on his left also fell away; one of the businesses had a tiny parking area. A security light shone from a concrete loading dock the size of a small porch.

If it hadn't been for the security light, Cole might not have even noticed the car.

It wasn't near the business. It was parked under some trees at the edge of the vacant lot—not really in the alley, but not exactly in the lot either. It had seen better days, the rear window broken and taped over with what appeared to be black plastic garbage bags.

Cole wouldn't have thought much about it if *he* hadn't just been taping a black plastic garbage bag to seal out light. If Royal hadn't been on his mind only a moment ago.

And if the security light hadn't been bright enough to show that this plastic was mounted from the *inside*.

So he stopped and took a closer look.

He was right; the plastic was plastered solidly against the inside of the glass. Not only that, but none of the glass was broken at all—it was completely intact.

Cole circled the car. It was a two-door, dark-colored Civic—probably black, although light played tricks with color at night—well over ten years old. It had been in a wreck at some point; the passenger side door had a rippled, limp look, as if it had been caved in and then hammered out. Both back side windows had been carefully covered from the inside as well.

Cole put a hand on the hood.

It was warm.

Cole looked around to make sure he was alone. He occasionally carried a jimmying rod in his trunk, under the spare—but he didn't like to. Eighteen-year-old guys got stopped often enough by cops just for being eighteen. What he *did* have at the moment was a crumpled wire hanger; it didn't work quite as easily but could usually be made to do the job, especially with older cars like this.

He went back to the Vickery Moe parking lot, to his own car, and got the hanger. Cole had had a lot of practice at this sort of thing; it took only a moment, and he had the Civic's door open.

The interior light came on. He dropped the hanger and quickly slid into the driver's seat. Then he leaned around to look in the back.

More black garbage bags were heaped on the floorboard, along with a roll of duct tape. A dark-colored pile of bedding took up most of the backseat itself; a zipper told Cole that the bedding was a sleeping bag.

He had no idea whether it was the one he'd seen in Royal's apartment. Yes, it appeared to be brown—but as far as Cole was concerned, one sleeping bag looked pretty much like another.

And he knew it was unlikely that the car belonged to

Royal. Sunlight was difficult to seal out of any car, even with garbage bags and duct tape. Cole didn't see how any heme could survive a day in this jerry-rigged vehicle.

He leaned over and opened the glove compartment. There was a flashlight and some papers; he dug through the papers to find an insurance card.

The carrier was Kimberly Lynn Brandywine.

He was suddenly aware that he was very close to getting himself in a ton of trouble.

He put back the card, closed the glove box, and got out of the car. He pushed the lock down and was about to shut the door when he hesitated.

Why was the car parked out here, almost in a no-man's-land? Wouldn't an omni have left it closer to the loading dock, or on the street out front?

He checked up and down the alley again. No one coming.

He stooped and pulled the latch that opened the trunk. When he heard it pop, he shut the driver's door quietly and walked quickly around.

Another glance to make sure he was alone, and he lifted the trunk lid.

A small light came on, dimly lighting the contents: A pack rat's nest of clothing, towels, newspapers. A roll of black garbage bags. Empty water bottles. Scissors. A paint-spattered hammer, a screwdriver. Lightbulbs. Batteries.

Nothing worrisome. Nothing scary. Nothing dangerous. Only things any omni might toss in. Cole had seen plenty of omni cars loaded with junk like this in the floorboard and backseat and trunk.

But these were also things a heme would carry in case of emergency. Cole had many of the same items in *his* trunk, although not thrown all together like this.

What to do? He couldn't stand here indefinitely, poking through some omni's car. Kimberly Brandywine might come back. And she might have people with her.

On the other hand, if Royal had borrowed or stolen the car, he was obviously sleeping in it. And if it were his, he'd be back sometime in the next couple of hours, before the sun started to rise.

He might have even *already* come back. Cole realized—a little late—that there were several small dark places around him, where one person could be hiding and watching unseen. The space between the Dumpster and the loading dock. The recessed doorways all along the alley.

Cole shut the trunk as if he wasn't even thinking

about being watched and headed back down the alley. As soon as he was out of the parking lot, he stepped quickly aside, into the shadows. He would see anyone following before they saw him.

He waited long moments.

No one came.

He had planned to feed now. But the thought that he and Sandor and Gordo might have been followed all this way gave him a creepy, spied-on feeling.

Cole wanted to know whether or not this car was Royal's. He wanted to know *tonight*.

He moved into a recessed doorway under a rickety-looking fire escape, his back against the door: He could see the Civic from here, but no one would be able to see him. He'd grab a quick feed first thing tomorrow evening, when he went to select an omni to take to the Vickery Moe for the Siege of Gordo. For now he'd watch the car. If he just knew whether the stray were tailing them, he could start figuring out what to do about it.

He heard traffic in the distance, the faraway slam of a door—but there was no movement in the parking lot or alley. The car sat under the trees, just another piece of the background. It had an almost abandoned look— except for the odd, carefully applied window coverings.

Any heme who sheltered in that car would be living life on the edge in a way that the Colony hemes no longer had to. He would be desperate, cornered, afraid. And utterly, utterly alone.

That might explain why Royal would follow them for hundreds of miles over several nights. But it wouldn't explain why he'd never made any kind of contact. If he was lonely, why not approach them?

The intimidating talk, the finger guard—maybe, Cole thought, it was all of a piece. He had seen plenty of omni wannabes posture in that same way, and it had always seemed to Cole that they were trying to make up for the impotence of their everyday lives. Maybe he'd let an emotional knee-jerk reaction keep him from recognizing the same thing in Royal.

He checked his watch. Twenty minutes had passed. Still no sign of anyone.

Light, Cole thought grimly, wouldn't be the only problem for anyone who tried to get through a day in that car. It was June now, and summer heat would turn the Civic into an oven within a few hours. With windows rolled up and plastic in place, a heme would essentially be locking himself into an airless coffin.

306

Not to mention that it would take a lot of work to follow someone from eastern Pennsylvania to Ohio to West Virginia to Maryland. It had seemed unlikely back in Ohio. It seemed almost impossible now.

But Cole wanted to be sure. He shifted his weight again and leaned one shoulder against the doorway, waiting.

Another half hour passed.

An hour.

Cole decided he'd give it till five A.M. The light would start growing soon after. After five o'clock there wouldn't be enough time for anyone to get himself shut away in that little torture chamber.

When the hour came, Cole knew the sun had started its clockwork climb to the horizon. Still, he waited a few more uneasy minutes. Just to be positive.

At 5:10, he looked up. The piece of sky visible overhead was still black, but with a slightly faded look. It was hard to tell much, in cities.

He grew still, paying attention to his body. Yes. He felt a slight discomfort, as if his skin were dry and slightly chapped. The light was changing.

The hotel was two blocks away.

He left his shadowy recess and walked quickly back down the alley. When he turned the corner onto the sidewalk next to the Vickery Moe, he finally had a clear view of the eastern sky.

A portion of it was dulled by rain clouds, but the rest had a definite grayish tone.

There was still time, he knew, and he didn't like to run—it attracted attention—but he walked very, *very* quickly up the sidewalk to the hotel's front door.

He'd mention the car to Sandor sometime when Gordo wasn't around. Still, he felt he could safely put the question of Royal aside for now. He was glad; tomorrow looked to be a long night.

CHAPTER TWENTY-FOUR

IN his room, Cole found that his skin—especially his arms and face—was slightly pink and tender, like an omni's mild sunburn. It would take time to go away, he knew.

He'd planned to take a shower before bed, but the thought of water hitting his skin made him wince. He changed into his usual shorts and T-shirt and went to bed, deciding not to read first. He wanted to be fresh tonight, be alert.

Once in bed, though, he had trouble sleeping. His skin was tingling as it healed, and he kept thinking about Bess, and about the Old World heme, the one Johnny had trapped. Cole knew they both must have felt this same dry discomfort turn to tenderness—but then *they'd* had to endure its quick growth into pain.

What courage—or despair—Bess must have had to climb that ladder into sunlight! Opening the hatch to expose herself to bright, bright sky. And—suffering and surely blinded by then—she'd had to scale the last remaining rungs. Drag herself onto the roof. Somehow cross it, all the way to the edge.

On that day he, Cole, had barely made it out the front door before he'd turned back. Hadn't been able to get down even one of the steps that would take him to her.

But what he'd told Gordo that night in Castile was true. He hadn't really thought it through logically before, but now he did, and he knew it was a fact: Nobody could have made it out there. Not even Johnny could retrieve another heme from full sun. Whatever drove Bess that day was something no one else had. Whatever it was, it had pushed her headlong, past human endurance, to its goal.

Cole had been curled on his side, but now he rolled onto his back. *Surely*, he was thinking, *by the time she was on the sidewalk, she was unconscious and out of pain*. It made sense that she would be.

He hoped so.

But the Old World heme—what kind of animal terror

took *him* over, trapped, aware, with no escape from light?

Cole winced as he adjusted the covers over his chest. He had to admit now that—no matter what he had promised himself, no matter what he had told Johnny— he couldn't do anything so cruel to Gordo. Whether he could do it to a stranger he didn't know, but he could not do it to Gordo.

No, he would have to make sure it didn't come to *that*.

He lay staring at the ceiling. A siren sounded in the distance, but it was very far away and soon faded. Muffled voices moved down the hall—two men, laughing and talking. Had to be omnis; it was late morning and light out.

As they passed, Cole turned his head; his nose had caught their faint, salt-and-soap scent.

That was odd. Usually his sense of smell wasn't that acute—not enough to detect omnis through a closed door. Must be the airflow in this old building.

His skin was beginning to feel better. According to the clock, it was full daytime. The only sound now was the window unit, which might look like an antique but was proving to be a workhorse, its icy breath one long unwavering blast so that the room was almost cold.

Cole shut his eyes and made an effort to clear his mind. And after a little longer, he finally managed to fall asleep.

Almost immediately he found himself in a patchwork of dreams—quick-flashing scenes of desire. He dreamed of combining, of omnis he had known, of soft, fragile, sweet-smelling skin under his hands and lips and tongue. The flashes gradually melted into a dream of sex—sex from long ago, and in his dream he had to peel, unfasten, burrow, just to get down to the girl's bare skin.

It was all quite vivid; the delay, the frustration, his trembling fingers loosening the last layer of lace and strings and straps so that he almost burst just from the sudden sight of nakedness released.

He roused to wakefulness, the experience so real that the odor of talc and stale sweat seemed to linger in his nostrils.

He was sweating now.

Cole kicked off the covers and lay under the cooling air. This was probably a weird aftereffect of sun. Even the pillow under his head felt hot.

He pulled it out, turned it over, plumped it up. Put it back.

This time when he dozed off he dreamed of an omni he'd kept for a while in the early days. She'd stayed with him, in full awareness of what he was, and sometimes he would deliberately hold off feeding until he was wild with it.

In the dream he pushed her up against a wall, put his hands flat on the wall on either side of her, trying to prolong the moment, play with her—he acted as if he were about to bite her, then pulled back so that she could just feel the scratch of his teeth. Nip at her but not break the skin. She knew what was coming and caught her breath; and at that tiny noise he lost it, lost himself completely to the feed.

He woke to find his hands curled in fists, gripping the sheets.

And he remembered how he'd smelled the omnis in the hall.

It was almost as if . . . well, as if he was starting to feel the barest wisp of Thirst. Thirst always took over the mind before it started to work on the body.

But it *couldn't* be—not so soon. He'd only gone two

313

nights without a feed. All right, it had been a long time since he'd missed more than a single night, and even longer since he'd actually felt Thirst; but he remembered, *remembered distinctly*—no mere two-night lapse had ever brought it on. No, it always took four nights. Three at the very least.

He was *not* mistaken.

He could *count*, for God's sake.

And anybody would have weird dreams if they were gearing up for a stressful night ahead, the way Cole was. Then, too, he'd been preoccupied with Royal. On top of that, he knew he'd cut it too close earlier—risked a touch of light just because he'd wanted to be sure about the stray.

All that would be enough to make anybody have strange and vivid dreams.

He got up and went to the bathroom. Checked the tape on the window. Checked the locks. Tried to read a bit but couldn't. Finally he put down the book and shut his eyes.

Almost immediately he dreamed of a simple overpowering without thought of restraint or consequences—of attacking an omni in the open, from behind, on a city street. In the dream he took no care but tore the flesh so that blood ran out of the corners of his mouth, too great a flow to contain. He didn't stop even after the pulse slowed and the kill drooped in his arms. When there was nothing left, he dropped the empty and useless husk in the middle of the sidewalk and walked away.

What woke him this time was need: every corner of his brain and body pounding with it, every cell insisting that the emptiness be filled.

It began to fade a little as he came back to consciousness, and by the time he opened his eyes it had half dulled.

But after one disoriented moment he realized that he was standing at the door, barefoot in his shorts and T-shirt, hand on the knob.

With that he knew. It *was* Thirst.

Something had gone terribly wrong. Something inside him must have changed, to make him feel this way after only two missed nights.

Or—or—maybe *he* had changed it. He was the one who'd trained his body to expect nightly intake. He had been priming his metabolism for decades.

He'd had such contempt for Gordo, unable to resist a few drops of blood because he was used to regular feeds. Cole had assumed it was a matter of will—well, maybe it was in Gordo's case, but Cole hadn't even considered that it could be a matter of one's body adapting to regular use.

It would be ironic—if all the years of caution and control, far from keeping him sharp and fit, had instead been softening him up.

Well, he *wasn't* Gordo. He'd experienced Thirst plenty of times in the past. He knew how to handle it—especially at this early stage, when it had just begun.

He didn't try to go back to bed this time. As long as he was awake he was sure he could keep the need pushed down. It still licked at him from inside, but now that he knew what it was he had the reins on. At this point, Thirst was merely a craving that hadn't fully blossomed.

The trouble was that if he was feeling it, there was no question that Gordo—uncontrolled, inexperienced Gordo—must be feeling it, too.

CHAPTER TWENTY-FIVE

HE started to call Sandor's cell phone to warn him, but he wasn't sure of the number. He thought about banging on the wall, but that would alarm Sandor to no purpose. There were windows at each end of the hall, and Sandor couldn't come over to see what he wanted.

So he waited. He watched the clock, and when it was time he peeled a corner of the tape from the curtain to make doubly sure.

The sky was dark. Cole could hear thunder in the distance, but no rain was falling.

He was already dressed. He felt hyperaware, hyperalert, as if he moved in a slipstream of time that was ticking a few seconds ahead of everything around him. But he had himself under complete control. And before he did *anything* else, he had to get Gordo's feed. He had to do it quickly.

Next door, Sandor looked a little disturbed when he answered Cole's knock.

"He's in the shower," he said, as Cole stood impatient in the doorway. "He's been in there for almost an *hour* with the water running. He doesn't answer when I knock. Before I was even up, he was—"

"I'm going to get him a feed right now," Cole interrupted. "You keep him here—whatever you do, don't let him out of this room. It's hitting him already," he said, to Sandor's confused look. "He's standing under cold water in there. He's fighting it. But I guarantee he's going to blow in a bit. Keep him here, and I'll be right back."

"Do you want me to go instead?"

"No. I'll be quicker." He would, too—he was in the grip of a sharp, crisp urgency. Every one of his senses was hungry and on the prowl.

"Cole—"

But Cole was already gone.

He took the steps three at a time and was in the car in less than a minute.

And he quickly found what he needed, less than five

blocks away—the plan would have been a good one, if he hadn't screwed up this one point.

She was older than Gordo would like, he was sure—but she would do. She was in her thirties, with a rather hard face but with laugh lines that made her almost seem as if she were still pretty. She wore white shorts with stilettos and a flannel shirt with the tails tied tightly just under her breasts. She was thin but sturdy, and very tan, with wiry muscled arms and pale hair that looked white over her bronzed skin.

He thought about feeding from her himself, just a *little* bit—it wouldn't take long at all, he told himself—but he knew she needed to be full and intact. It might be hard to get the kid off her once he got started.

A cigarette poked out of her mouth at a right angle; she was surrounded by a stagnant swirl of smoke. Cole was glad—one more brick to add to his wall of self-control.

He paid her in advance and took her back to the hotel. She was a talker; in those five blocks he learned that her name was Crystal and that she wasn't originally from Maryland but from a small town in Virginia. She'd run track in ninth grade but dropped out of high school when she was sixteen. She had a little girl back in Virginia, living with Crystal's mother and stepdad. She was hoping to go home for Thanksgiving.

The few remarks he made were soothing, low, and quite controlled.

At the Vickery Moe, Cole didn't even try Sandor and Gordo's door, knowing that Sandor would have locked it. He pounded a couple of times on the door frame, Crystal patient beside him.

When Sandor let them in, Gordo was just coming out of the bathroom. The kid was fully dressed, but for once he hadn't attended at all to his hair. It was still wet, and pieces were stuck together in damp clumps.

He saw Crystal and stopped in his tracks—the intense focus, Cole thought, of a dog that just spotted a rabbit.

After a few stunned seconds, Gordo managed to pull his gaze away from her. He turned accusingly to Cole. "What's she doing here?" he demanded.

"She's for you," Cole said.

"What do you mean?"

"She's a gift."

"I don't want any 'gift.'"

But Cole saw Gordo's eyes flick back to Crystal. "Yes,

you do," Cole said, calm in certainty. This would be over within minutes.

"Where did you find her?" Gordo said, aiming a glare at Cole now.

"What difference does it make?"

"I want to know why she came here with you."

Crystal spoke up. "Hi, sweetie," she said kindly, as if Gordo were eight instead of eighteen. "I'm Crystal. What's your name?"

Gordo scowled down at the floor.

"Gordon," Cole told her.

"It's all right, Gordon," Crystal told him. She moved over and sat on the closest bed. "Come sit down." She patted the spot beside her. "I'm not going to bite you."

Sandor evidently knew it was about to end. "I'll be in the hall," he whispered in Cole's ear, and Cole heard the door click softly as he stepped outside.

Gordo shook his head. "I don't want her," he told Cole. But Cole could hear the panic edging his voice.

"You *do* want her," Cole said. "And if you don't do it now, you're going to create a mess. Just like you did with your *girlfriend*," he added pointedly.

"Oh, my," Crystal said softly. "What happened with

your girlfriend, love?"

This time when Gordo's eyes went back to her, they locked on. And he wasn't staring at her face or body, Cole noticed—no, the kid was full-out hemovore for once, entranced with the curve of skin between her jaw and shoulder.

Now, Cole thought. Now he's going to do it.

But Gordo turned his head away.

"God," Cole said in disgust, "you've got no instincts at all. You're a freak of nature."

He had himself under tight control, but he pulled that control even tighter and stalked over to her, pasting on a smile that felt wolfish to him but that seemed to enthrall Crystal. "He's just shy," Cole told her soothingly as he held out his hand, and she, still caught in his gaze, let him pull her to her feet. Now he stepped behind her, so that he could watch Gordo over her shoulder.

"Oh no," said Gordo as Cole pulled his necklace out from under his shirt.

"She's pretty sturdy," Cole told him, lining up the point against her neck. "And you're pretty empty. You could probably go to as much as thirty."

"Thirty what?" Crystal asked.

"Don't do it," Gordo said, his voice scaling up. "I'm warning you."

Cole stuck his cross into her neck.

Almost instantly that metallic scent curled into his nostrils and then everything seemed to happen at once. He heard Crystal give a faint cry; he saw the dark red drop welling up, felt his fingers tightening on her shoulder as the drop burst its boundaries and fell into a trickle.

And then Gordo was on her.

Cole stepped back. He was sweating again, his breath coming in quick puffs. He turned his back on Gordo's feed, and, with jerky movements, forced himself to walk across the room. He found himself standing in front of the window, sucking in deep breaths. The plastic curtain had been pulled aside, and he suddenly realized that he was standing exposed to view, the lights in the room clearly visible from the darkness outside. He began to fumble for the edge of the curtain, to draw it closed.

Finally he heard a rustle, and he knew: Gordo had stopped on his own.

The kid had potential. If he'd just stop being such a pain in the ass.

"Wow." That was Crystal, her voice a little weak but

323

breathless with wonder, and Cole allowed himself to turn around.

"Feel better now?" he asked Gordo.

Gordo fell back to sit on the bed. "You're the devil," he told Cole, sounding suddenly weary. "You know that?"

"I'm whatever I have to be. Do you want her for anything else?"

"No. I'm tired."

Cole studied him. He looked about as exhausted as Cole felt. "I imagine you are," Cole agreed, and then he turned to Crystal. "Come on, I'll take you back."

She didn't seem puzzled at all by the sudden change of plan. Just . . . awed. By the whole experience.

When they stepped into the hall, Sandor was waiting, lounging back against the wall. "All done?" he asked cheerfully. "I can take Miss Crystal if you'd like to stay with Gordo."

"No," said Cole. "I need to go." He took Crystal by the elbow and started herding her down the hall.

"Cole," Sandor said, "are you—?"

"Yes," Cole told him without looking back.

CHAPTER TWENTY-SIX

COLE noticed that his hands were shaking now—it was difficult to get the key into the lock of his car door. Crystal stood quiet but pale, waiting and watching him with an oddly reverent look.

"Mind if I smoke?" she asked, as soon as she got in. For a second he thought he could hear her pulse under the flannel of her blouse, but he realized that was silly—of course he couldn't.

"Please do." He would get her back safely and untouched. Gordo had taken too much; she could not hold up to another feed.

They were just a few blocks from where he'd picked her up; it would take only minutes to get her back and seconds to find somebody else nearby.

That was good; even snarls of cigarette smoke couldn't

obscure all the lovely, rich, life-filled blood vessels that were feeding oxygen throughout her body.

"You guys are angels, aren't you?" he heard Crystal ask. She sounded very wise.

Cole looked at her, and for a brief second he could really *see* her, a human being behind the blood vessels and the smoke. So pathetic. Her little girl. Her short life. All soon to be forgotten.

"Yes," he said.

"I thought so." She looked out the window. "Why did you choose me?"

Cole thought for a moment. He did not particularly believe in God. If there was one, Cole had been cut off from him forever. Cole didn't have to answer to God, and never would.

But this woman . . . he had a sudden urge to give her something. Something she could use—belief, hope, a sense of worth—she could likely use those. He could almost see them filling her now—just because she thought she'd met an angel—putting light in her face, squaring her shoulders.

So he didn't bat an eye at pretending to be God's messenger. "God loves you, Crystal. No matter what, he loves you. And," he added as a thought occurred to him, "he wants you to take care of your little girl."

She nodded, positively beaming.

He pulled over to the curb near the place where he'd first spotted her. She reeled a little when she got out of the car, but he felt it would be unwise to touch her right now, so he did not offer any help. When the door shut behind her, he let out the breath he'd been holding, nice and slow and controlled.

Fat drops splatted on the windshield. Crystal walked around the nearby corner and was gone.

Cole waited another moment, then got out.

In that moment the drops had turned into a down-pour. Within seconds water was running in rivulets down his face. He ignored it and stepped onto the side-walk, looking around.

There were only a few omnis scattered along the streets now, but it seemed to him as if they were *everywhere*; even in the wet air their salty skin smells and delicate blue veins seemed to be leaping out at him.

Most of them were heading away, trying to get out of the rain—a denim dress ducking into a brown sedan, a pink skirt scurrying into a doorway, a yellow rain slicker bounding to cross the street like a gazelle—but one was completely in the open, a gift in the middle of the sidewalk.

Dark shirt with a low curving neckline. He could see the white of her face and neck and chest. Oh, she set his pulse pounding.

Because she was coming directly toward him. Her only shelter was a black umbrella and a man's Windbreaker, unzipped, hood up. The streetlight behind her turned the rain into individual drops, a curtain of tiny pellets falling to Earth.

Dark, softly curling hair under the hood. Like Bess— she was like Bess.

She sensed someone standing in front of her and glanced up. Her step faltered. He must be in a wild state to be able to halt someone in midstride with just the force of his stare.

For a brief moment her eyes were fastened to his face. It had been so long since he'd had this much desire for anything—she was thin in faded jeans, but her breasts were full against the light lining of the Windbreaker. Her curls stopped just under her chin.

Whatever she saw in him, it didn't scare her; she

dropped her gaze to the sidewalk and moved forward again.

Closer. Closer. Brown eyes big in her face—*Bess*, he thought wildly, and then: No, he could not tell the color of her eyes from here. He took another deep, controlled breath—but this one refused to be held in check. It escaped, and as it fled, Thirst swelled over the boundaries he'd so carefully set, expanding into the space his breath had occupied and twining its way deep into his gut.

She had already curled around the hollow in his middle. Now she tugged him toward her as she passed. He just had time to think that he *must* restrain himself, that he could not do this in public, when his body took over and he was after her, one hand automatically reaching for his cross.

One splashing step, and in that step he could actually *feel* the last shreds of control loosen and drop away.

His hand dropped the cross and shot out to grab the back of her Windbreaker, jerking it toward him while he flung his other arm around her shoulders and brought his weight to bear on her back. In the same second he was at her neck.

He bit down. Hard.

A sweet burst and flow, and then everything swelled in one slow wave. The richness filling his mouth. Her slow breath sweeping through her body. Her soft curls turning wet against his cheek. The warmth of her skin under the rain's chill.

It was ridiculously easy, so rich, so pulsing that he hardly even had to swallow.

He sank his teeth in till the trickle became a gush, so fast that he couldn't keep it under control. He choked and sputtered. He couldn't breathe.

But he couldn't let go either. It was wonderful, to take what he wanted, all he wanted, without thought. It'd been so long—the wild, uncaring need.

His pulse, his heart, his tongue, his throat, all hummed with joy, and he was only vaguely aware when her hand, still clutching the open umbrella, slowly fell to her side. Rain pelted his shoulders. It ran down his cheeks, dripped from the end of his nose. He was wonderfully overloaded, flooded with pleasure; he knew this type of omni, his favorite, he ran his hand over the flat belly, and the breasts that swelled out from the rib cage and spilled so deliciously over his fingers—Bess had been like that, although she had never allowed him to touch her; she'd hated him too much—he dug his teeth in even deeper. . . .

It was so easy, to take whatever you wanted.

She swayed a little and began to droop as if her knees had gone to jelly, and a part of him began to be aware. Inside, part of him knew how far he'd gone.

A few more seconds and he could no longer ignore the thinning of the flow in his mouth. He was reluctant to let go—letting go would mean that he had to face what he'd done. But his Thirst was dying, and his stomach wasn't used to being so uncomfortably full.

As soon as he raised his head, the wounds stopped bleeding and the girl sagged in his arms.

Oh, God.

He clutched her tighter. As long as he made her part of him, they were both safe. His physical need was gone, but he was completely off balance inside now. He couldn't think.

The girl was completely limp, and suddenly very heavy.

Okay. Okay. He *had* to think. Had to figure out what to do next.

The rain was slackening already; it had been only a shower, tailor-made to get everyone off the street long enough to hide his lapse. He did not look around to see who might be watching; he raised his head just enough to find the darkened windows of a closed palm reader's shop a few steps away.

He half carried, half dragged her to its recessed doorway. As he lowered her to the ground, he saw her eyelids flutter.

She was alive.

He crouched and cautiously felt for a pulse. There, but barely. Weak. Too fast. Her Windbreaker had fallen open; her shirt was a tank top, clinging to those breasts, and he had to look away. Omnis and their black. Why did they always wear black?

He turned his head, furtively now, looking around.

Down the street, two omnis, two males in jeans, walking away from him. In the other direction the sidewalk was empty except for a quick glimpse of a dark figure stepping out of sight into one of the buildings. Cole squinted through the patches of dark and light on the sidewalk, but nothing moved; whoever it was must have gone into one of the businesses.

No one had seen. And he couldn't linger another second: He had to get out of here.

He stood and started walking away.

After a few paces he realized suddenly that he didn't know where he was going. And then he remembered that his car was in the opposite direction. Everything was crazy. He couldn't *think*.

He looked around wildly, spotted his car, and headed toward it, head down now. He had to force himself not to run; he tried to keep his pace even but brisk. Nothing to stand out.

He hadn't even locked the car doors.

He slid in—and then hesitated. The doorway where he'd left her was ahead on his right. If he hadn't known what that small dark heap was, he wouldn't have guessed. No one had seen her yet. No one would, unless they passed her. Should he go back and get her, take her to a hospital?

No. He must leave this place—he'd go back to the hotel and call 911. No, no—they'd know where to look for him then—no, he'd use Sandor's cell. He'd make sure that his voice didn't show anything. He'd hang up as soon as he'd said where she was, and no one would ever know.

333

The address—what was the address? He couldn't see, couldn't see; there were too many drops on the windshield—okay, the wipers—he started the car and turned on the wipers, and the drops swept away like magic. He was a mess right now, he knew—the past two days, and now this.

His eyes searched the building next to him for a number—2135. What street? Shit, what street? He'd have to read it from the corner street sign.

He pulled out and a moment later turned on the headlights. As he passed, he looked out the window to see her, a huddled lump on the concrete.

He drove away, watching the doorway that marked her body in the rearview mirror. It disappeared in the dark as if sinking into a current.

CHAPTER TWENTY-SEVEN

ON the way back he started shivering; he was cold, his clothes were wet through, and though it must still be early in the evening, he was exhausted. And the girl—he was weak now, and the connections wouldn't go away. He'd thought he was in danger of being dead inside, but he'd been wrong.

Bess. He could still feel the raw emotion of loving her, how it raked over him till it was almost painful. His fingers had been on the smooth skin of her arm, and he'd thought how at this moment it was growing older, how it was shriveling—so slowly that he could not see it, but shriveling nonetheless, and how the hair floating in curly tendrils would turn lank and white like gauze. The hand in his would turn into a bony claw, and the eyes that were now sharp and precise would become vacant and confused.

Either that, or she would die and leave only a worn path through the synapses in his brain, a path that would disappear from lack of use. Memories didn't last intact; he'd already known that, even then.

Every second he'd thought, a knot of panic growing in his chest, of how she was drifting further away.

He'd turned, so that he could look down at her, still nestled against him. She was watching him—many times afterward he had wondered how his face must have looked to her at that moment—but he couldn't move his eyes from the skin under the curve of her jaw. It looked smooth, white, cold like a marble statue. But when he'd bent over her it was fleeting softness, fleeting warmth that made his breath leave him in one short sigh.

When he was done, he'd raised his head and, for some odd reason, couldn't quite bring himself to look at her face.

Bess. She'd taken over every beat of his heart like an emotional Thirst. Even the smallest bared expanse of skin had burned into his brain, the slightest brush of her hand had clutched the breath out of his body, the steadiness of her clear eyes looking up into his had melted his life into hers. He'd been as bad as Gordo, telling himself he could push it all away, trying through sheer will to force it not to exist, but the truth was that even after a hundred and seventy years of grief and love, he still didn't know how to disconnect himself.

Sandor opened the door of 211 almost before Cole could knock. "There you are," he said, obviously relieved. "Are you all right?"

"I need your phone," Cole said, holding out his hand.

Sandor studied him for a moment—just a bare moment—then dug in his pocket and handed Cole the phone. He did not show surprise. He did not ask why.

He did not go back into the room, either. He glanced back over his shoulder and then stepped out into the hall, keeping one hand on the doorknob and his eyes on Cole, alert.

Cole pressed the 9, the 1, the 1 again—then hesitated. He wasn't used to cell phones.

Sandor reached over and pushed a button for him. "It's dialing now," he said.

Cole held the phone to his ear. As soon as he heard a woman's voice on the other end, he said quickly,

"There's a girl passed out in a doorway. You need to send an ambulance." He heard himself give the address, then repeat it, very clearly. "Send an ambulance," he said again.

He didn't know how to hang up, so he handed the phone back to Sandor.

Sandor pressed a button. He stuck the phone back in his pocket. Then he gave Cole a silent, measuring look, as if to say, "What next?"

Cole just stood there, arms dangling at his sides. All purpose seemed to have drained out of him. What *was* next? What *was* there to do?

"You seem a bit shell-shocked, my friend," Sandor said. "And you look like something the cat dragged in. Why don't you go to your room, get cleaned up, maybe take a little nap?"

But Cole remembered now. "Gordo," he said, and was surprised to hear that his voice was suddenly hoarse.

For answer, Sandor held the door open just enough for Cole to see in.

Gordo was sitting on one of the beds. He'd propped a pillow against the headboard and was leaning comfortably against it, legs stretched in front of him, watching

338

TV. He glanced over at the door's movement, saw Cole, and, after one abashed moment, lifted his hand in an embarrassed greeting.

It was as if nothing had happened.

Sandor pulled the door shut. "You were right; it was good for him to feel Thirst. We had a nice talk while you were out. And now it's my turn to be on duty. Go on," he urged. "You can check in with us later. Go home, mother hen."

It took Cole a moment to process all this. He had the feeling of something heavy slowly dropping away. He'd always thought of relief as a sudden thing, but now he only gradually took everything in: the completed call, Gordo on the bed, Sandor's words.

He was back safe, and his charge was safe as well, and Sandor had taken over for him.

Back in room 213, the air-conditioning was still running full blast, and his damp clothes made him shiver. He went into the bathroom and stripped them off while running hot water.

In the shower, he thought at first he had hurt something inside by overfeeding on the omni; he thought it was a pain working its way up from his chest. And then he felt his face crumple, and he knew. He leaned against the steamy tile while the water poured over him and great, gulping sobs wrenched their way out of his chest. He was grateful for the rushing water, which covered every sound.

All in all, it was a very odd night.

Cole fell instantly to sleep as soon as he hit the bed—a delicious nothingness of dreamless sleep.

From the depths of that nothingness, his mind barely registered a slight noise, a soft click—but it wasn't enough to really wake him. What woke him was a strange pressure, like a finger in the middle of his chest. Even that didn't rouse him fully; he felt the discomfort, and sleepily tried to roll over, away from it— but the pressure concentrated and grew into pain, as if someone were pressing him down, trying to pin him to the mattress.

His eyes flew open to yellowish light. Someone had turned on the bedside lamp. And in a split second he saw it all. A ghostly face hovered over him—Royal, one skinny black-clad arm raising the paint-spattered hammer Cole had seen in the Civic's trunk.

There was no time to feel fear—just to glimpse Royal's coolly determined face and the descending hammer—before a crack of pain in Cole's chest exploded into a crushing suffocation that shot into his arms, his neck. Everything was suffocating.

The last thing he thought was that he had completely overlooked this particular danger. And the last things he saw were Royal's eyes, inches away, peering into his own with steady, clinical interest.

CHAPTER TWENTY-EIGHT

THEN the pain was gone, and Cole was floating over a field filled with people. He drifted over the tops of their heads, thousands of them, as far as the eye could see, all moving slowly in the same direction. Not one of them looked up. The grass under their feet was a bright green that only comes in midspring when everything is fresh and new, well watered, hopeful, full of births and pleasant surprises.

As he floated lower and lower, he could make out more details: blond hair, brown, black, straight, kinky, braided; clothing of all shades and styles. Some people were barefoot, some high heeled; some wore scuffed boots or running shoes or sandals. He searched for a place to land, a place where he could gently and safely loft to earth, set both feet on that green grass and walk with the others.

But there was no room. They were all shifting, moving, and he could not keep up enough to find a place to land. He could only watch and feel as they passed him by and moved on. The peace of their passage was palpable, and it was real, as real as the light that shone among them.

He floated, heavy with sorrow and with joy, watching them pass. He understood now what heaven was. He was there on the edge but was unable to be part of it. It was a journey, not a place.

He could never go among them. He could never walk where they were walking.

Not in dreams. Not even in death.

CHAPTER TWENTY-NINE

AGONY drew him back. Fierce, sucking, as if his heart were being ripped out of his chest, and he felt his throat and jaws open in a soundless spasm.

It all contracted quickly into a tremendous surge of pain, punctuated by heartbeat after heartbeat that shot along his body in waves, bullying their way through with each scrape of his pulse.

He felt his lungs fill with air, tightening his chest as if a band were being screwed around it.

He wanted to go back and float over the fields again, but he couldn't; he was bolted and clamped by pain, flat on his back, unable to move or speak, unable to drift.

He did not know how long he lay like that. He was aware of familiar voices that he couldn't quite identify, speaking in words that he couldn't understand. It was all vaguely puzzling; and when the voices rose in gentle questioning tones, only to be followed by a hanging silence, he knew, in sorrow and frustration, that the silence was his to fill and he was falling short.

When he finally opened his eyes, Johnny was there. Johnny, beside him, looking down into his face.

Next to Johnny, Sandor. And now Gordo came into his field of vision too, as if he'd risen from a seat on Cole's right.

Cole felt a light pressure on his legs—a familiar pressure, of sheets and a blanket—and suddenly he remembered that he had seen heaven, and he opened his mouth to try to tell them.

But he was too tired. And it made no difference anyway.

"Are you with us, Cole?" Johnny asked.

Cole tried to nod. He couldn't, but somehow it was enough, because Sandor smiled and leaned down, his words pouring over Cole.

"Your heart seems to be better now, and your sternum's healed. It's very good you're not omni; you'd be lying there for weeks. Well, actually, if you were omni, you'd be dead, wouldn't you? In any case, you must save your strength. I have to tell you that it was quite a shock to come in here and find you lying in bed with a

345

two-foot fence picket driven into your chest."

"Royal," Cole tried to whisper, but all that came out was a wheeze.

Still, Sandor understood. "Of course. Who else? Cole, he pulled the window curtain completely down before he took off! If Gordo hadn't come over to talk to you, you'd be . . . well, you'd be—"

"Don't worry about it right now," Johnny said. "We'll make sure nothing like this happens again."

"Oh, yes," Sandor said with enthusiasm, "when I find that little bastard I will crush him like a fly. I tell you, in Boravia we know how to deal with *strigoi*. I've been telling Gordo that this is what happens when one doesn't belong to a community—one ends up getting one's information from bad B movies. I hope you have learned a lesson here, Gordo."

"You sound like Cole," Gordo said, but his tone was that of the reasonable Gordo rather than the pouting teenager. "Everything's a lesson."

"Well," Sandor said, "Cole is laid up for a little while, isn't he? And so I must step in to fill his shoes." He bent closer to Cole. "I tell you, Cole," he said in a stage whisper, "if we had gotten Gordo a dog, none of this would have happened."

PART THREE

The Heart of the Colony

CHAPTER THIRTY

THE following evening they were able to start the drive home.

Cole was no longer in pain, but his body had exhausted its reserves of strength. Perhaps it was something to do with his blood pooling and clotting for hours as he lay on the bed, or perhaps his poor body had to work extra hard to get everything pumping and moving to all its cells again. In any case, Johnny had stolen one of the Vickery Moe pillows and Cole leaned against it, stretched out as much as he could in the backseat of the Accord.

Gordo was in the back too, crammed up against the other door. Cole felt bad for him but couldn't summon the energy to sit up.

They'd decided to make the journey in one night.

Johnny had flown down to Baltimore, but he wanted to ride back with Cole. He sat in the front passenger seat while Sandor drove, and he kept a close eye on the rearview mirror.

"There's no way to find out exactly where Royal has gone," he told Cole without looking around, "but I can guarantee you one thing: he's *not* following us now."

"I don't understand him," Cole said. "If he wanted to do this, why wait till now? And where did he come from? I couldn't get anything out of him," he added, fretting. "I don't know how old he is. No clue who created him. Maybe someone from out of the country."

"It's always the foreigners, isn't it?" Johnny said dryly. "I don't think you have to look that far afield."

"There's no one here who would do something like that."

"No?"

"No," Cole said with certainty. "No one in the Colony."

"I was thinking about Bess."

Usually when someone else said her name, it was like a little jolt, as if he'd been pricked with a knife. He waited for a moment now, but the jolt never came.

"Think about it, Cole. She was different the last time she came in. She'd always been a bit snappish, eh? Not

350

inclined to accept her situation—even after, what? Sixty years? Then all of a sudden she comes in in a downright funk, refusing to speak to anyone. Wouldn't even look any of us in the face."

"She was angry with me."

"She was *always* angry with you. But didn't she seem different that last time?"

"Well, she was sad."

"She was *different*, lad. Suddenly different. That's a bit odd for one of us, isn't it? Doesn't it make you think something happened to her? That maybe she did something she didn't like, was dead set against? Something she'd always hated you for doing?"

Cole thought about it. Strange, to just pull the situation out and think about it as a theoretical problem, uncolored by guilt or shame.

"That's quite a deductive leap," he told Johnny. "To go from saying she was sad to saying she created a heme and abandoned him."

"Yes. But it's something to consider. A possibility."

There was a lot to consider, and plenty of time in the backseat to consider it. Cole did a lot of thinking on that long trip back.

So did Gordo, apparently.

Cole had fallen asleep somewhere around Philly. When he opened his eyes, he saw that Gordo was watching him.

"Where are we?" he asked Gordo sleepily.

"I think we're almost out of New Jersey."

Cole nodded. He didn't feel like trying to sit up.

"Hey. You awake?" Gordo asked.

"Yes."

"Is it okay if I tell you something?"

"Sure."

"I'm, um . . . sorry about what happened to you."

"So am I."

"It was awful. Your eyes were open."

"Really?" That must have been rather horrifying.

"Yeah. They didn't look real; they looked like glass. And that thing sticking out of your chest." Gordo shuddered. "I almost threw up."

"Good thing you didn't."

"I thought you were dead."

"You know hemes can't die."

"But you *looked* dead. And it was my fault."

"It wasn't your fault," Cole told him. "It was mine. I was careless."

"No, it was mine. I know it was. If I'd done everything like you told me to, he never would have . . . It wouldn't have happened."

"Maybe not, but the bottom line is that I misjudged. I was careless of my surroundings and made mistakes of timing—"

"Oh, you two," Sandor said from the front seat. "Fault fault fault, blame blame blame. Can't you just be kind to yourselves? Really, either one of you could easily beat yourself senseless with guilt. It's very neurotic if you ask me."

Cole wanted to retort, but he couldn't think of anything to say. The annoying tiredness had begun to creep over him again. But there was something he wanted to know. "Gordo," he said, "Sandor said you came over to talk about something, the night you found me."

Gordo shrugged. "Well, yeah. I guess." He sounded embarrassed.

"What was it?"

"It wasn't important."

"I'd like to know. If you hadn't come in—how did you get in anyway?"

"The door was unlocked. I didn't try it, though—I

wouldn't do that. Sandor did."

"I was concerned," Sandor said from the front seat. "You'd had a rough evening. And then you didn't answer the door for hours. It's not like you to ignore people knocking."

Cole kept his attention on Gordo. "So what did you want to say?"

"I dunno." Gordo shifted in his seat. "It's just that . . . well . . . okay." He eyed Cole. "You told that lady I was a virgin, didn't you?"

It was an accusation, and for a moment Cole didn't understand.

Then he remembered: Crystal, the omni.

"Because it's not true," Gordo said with a wounded air. "You know?"

Cole *did* know, but he'd thought a helpful lie would make the evening go more smoothly. And it had. Crystal had approached Gordo gently and with patience.

"There's no way you could be, Gordo," Sandor commented. "Not after two weeks in the Building."

"I just don't think Cole should tell people something like that about me when it's not true."

Cole started to say he was sorry—but he wasn't. He

was glad he'd told that particular lie, and that Gordo had been compelled to come over and correct him.

"I won't do it again," he told Gordo instead. "And," he added, "I know it's not true."

Gordo nodded. "Damn straight," he said.

Cole was very weary now and closed his eyes for what felt like a second. But when he opened them the car was no longer on the freeway. It had stopped at a traffic light, and Gordo was talking to Sandor and Johnny.

". . . I could almost start to get used to living this way," Gordo was saying. "But it's dark when I go to bed, and it's dark when I wake up, and I can't get used to that."

"You can leave a light on," Cole said.

"He's awake again," Sandor commented.

"How are you feeling?" Johnny asked. "Any Thirst yet?"

"No," said Cole. "Not yet." He didn't like to think how much he'd taken from that girl.

"It's not the same," Gordo told Cole. "The colors are different than they are in sunlight."

"I guess I've forgotten."

"They look . . . fake."

Cole thought about it. In malls or stores, everything was too bright, lacking shadows. Bars and nightclubs were pools of dark punctuated by glaring neon or dim, recessed bulbs. "You can see sunlight in movies," he pointed out.

"It's still not the same. Sometimes I wish I could see a sunset. Just for a few seconds. I'd like to see all those colors. Do you think it would kill me?"

"No. I think it would tatter your skin and boil your brain, but I don't think it would kill you."

"Cole's back in form," Sandor remarked to Johnny.

Johnny just laughed.

CHAPTER THIRTY-ONE

IN Manhattan, Cole did not stay in four-and-a-half, but in one of Johnny's bedrooms. He spent the first evening on the patio, listening to speculation about Royal and letting Sandor and Gordo field questions about the trip.

"It's been eventful" was all he would say when anyone asked. He felt that was enough. He knew he'd be moving on soon—he still had a responsibility to Gordo, which he had no intention of shirking. In the meantime he was glad to see Sandor take the boy out of the Building to feed.

Good old Sandor. Now Cole learned, belatedly, that his friend had straightened out another screwup for him.

Alice was the one who told Cole. While the others

were deep in discussion, she came over and gently informed him that he must always consider carefully before using a Colony phone to dial 911. When he'd used Sandor's cell, Alice said, he'd left a trail connecting the unconscious girl directly to the Building.

It turned out that Sandor had known this. He hadn't said a word to Cole—just quietly set about taking care of the problem and let Cole go to his room to get some sleep.

When Alice went back to her seat, Cole was left feeling like an idiot. He couldn't help but consider the various ways Sandor had stepped in to pick up the slack for him in the past few days. And had always been there to do so, Cole saw now—even when Cole had thought of Gordo as his own exclusive burden. From the very beginning, too—God, Johnny had even laid it out clearly: There would be two of them, a safety net, a shared responsibility.

I've been stupid, Cole told himself. *Stupid, blind— and monstrously conceited.*

By the wee hours the talk on the patio was still going strong. Sandor and Gordo were back from their hunt. Cole had not moved from his cushioned wicker chair.

His feet were propped on a stool Nell had brought for him. He had nothing to say, nothing to add to the conversation, and he found himself drowsing.

But he wasn't willing to go to bed just yet. The familiar voices rising and falling around him made him feel immersed in a warm pool of companionship. He knew that if he opened his eyes, the feeling would disappear. It was nothing he could see, nothing he could touch, nothing he could hold on to. And he knew there was no real safety in it—no heme could ever truly be safe—just a sense that hands nearby were prepared to bear him up. He could falter, or fall—he could even break entirely— and hands lay ready to take on some of his load so that disaster *might* not follow his failures. And life *might* possibly even go on as if he hadn't broken at all.

The second evening, when the excitement had died down a little, Cole slipped out of Johnny's apartment to ride the everlasting elevator up to the fourth floor.

He still wasn't back to full strength yet and was sucking in air by the time he got to the landing at four-and-a-half. There he stood for a moment, catching his breath, peering up at the fifth-floor landing. The light was still on, of course. The walls glowed yellowish but bright.

He'd dreaded going up there. He had to admit: All these years he'd been wielding the mere *possibility* of going up there as a whip to punish himself. He'd thought that facing her shattered body again was the worst thing he could experience. He'd feared it; thought it would break him somehow.

But the idea of breaking didn't seem so concrete anymore. He'd cracked in more than one way lately, and yet he was still standing. And it now seemed that the worst thing about Bess had *already* happened to him.

It hadn't been when she'd fallen—he'd never really known for sure exactly when that happened anyway. And it wasn't seeing her afterward. Certainly that was a horrifying slice of time, a captured snapshot of emotion that remained crystal clear in his brain. But that was all it was. She was already gone by then. He'd already stood the worst that could happen, on the day she'd lain on that sunny sidewalk.

It had happened when he'd turned back.

That was the worst. All his will crumbling in the face of an impossible task, his body eaten by light and his brain slammed by an idea that was too monstrous to realize: His Bess was gone. That moment had knocked his world so completely off center that the fact he'd somehow remained standing through it slipped by without any notice.

It wasn't as though he'd made a choice to stand it. He just had, somehow.

He didn't know whether any sliver of her mind was still attached to the physical framework. Perhaps she was like a primitive creature that could experience light and dark without awareness of either. No matter what, she wouldn't know he was there—he was sure of it. Even if she were trapped floating above that river of people, as he had been, she wouldn't know he was in the room, sharing space with her still-living body.

But *he'd* know. *He'd* know she wasn't alone. *He'd* know that she was still connected to this earth.

And that he was connected to her.

I'm creating my own journey, he thought. Then he caught the railing with his hand and slowly started up.

AUTHOR'S NOTE

A "vampire" story seems an odd place to pay tribute to books about American pioneers, but so it is. Conrad Richter's Awakening Land Trilogy (*The Trees*, *The Fields*, and Pulitzer Prize–winning *The Town*) give me the same delight now that they did when I first read them in the 1980s. Richter's love and respect for his characters, their dialects, and their customs permeate his stories, and his descriptions of the old forests of the Northwest Territory bring a now-extinct landscape to life. And that is why Richter's writing—especially *The Trees* and *The Fields*—inspired parts of Cole's backstory in *Night Road*.